SAVING PEYTON

BROTHERHOOD PROTECTORS YELLOWSTONE
BOOK EIGHT

ELLE JAMES

TWISTED PAGE INC

SAVING PEYTON

BROTHERHOOD PROTECTORS
YELLOWSTONE BOOK #8

New York Times & USA Today
Bestselling Author

ELLE JAMES

Dedicated to my readers who n
by keeping me in the business I
love you all so much. Thank yo
Elle Jame

AUTHOR'S NOTE

Enjoy other military books by Elle James

Brotherhood Protectors Yellowstone

Saving Kyla (#1)

Saving Chelsea (#2)

Saving Amanda (#3)

Saving Liliana (#4)

Saving Breely (#5)

Saving Savvie (#6)

Saving Jenna (#7)

Saving Peyton (#8)

Saving Londyn (#9)

Visit ellejames.com for more titles and release dates

Join her newsletter at

https://ellejames.com/contact/

CHAPTER 1

CRUSHED beneath the weight of the man whose name she didn't know and didn't care to know, Peyton could barely breathe. She blinked in the dim lighting. Was the room hazy because she was about to pass out, or was it the drugs they'd kept her on throughout this nightmare that wouldn't end?

The air around her reeked of whiskey and sweat.

If she didn't get the man off her soon, she would surely die. Maybe that would be better than what she'd endured for...how long? She'd lost track of the days as she'd faded in and out of consciousness.

The hulk of a man shifted, rolled over onto his back and snorted loudly.

Peyton drew in a deep breath, her head swimming, her thoughts shifting like the prairie grasses, unable to hold still and focus.

One of her wrists was tied to a metal ring screwed

to the wall, the other had slipped free of the fabric they'd used to secure it. Her arm ached from being in the same position for so long.

With her free hand, she worked at the knot of what appeared to be an old T-shirt that had been ripped into strips and used to bind her to the wall in the squalid room. The mattress where she lay was bare of sheets and blankets. Cool air caressed her bruised body.

Peyton shivered as she continued to work the knot, her fingers fumbling, barely able to function. Finally, the knot loosened, and she pulled her wrist free. Wrapping both arms over her naked breasts, she lay shivering, needing to relieve her bladder, but afraid to move and wake the sleeping monster.

Moving slowly, she eased off the mattress, grabbed the man's jacket and slipped it over her shoulders, numb to the smell of his sweat. So many of the men who'd abused her offended her sense of smell. Even through the drug-induced haze, the stench of alcohol and sweat made her gag. Her only escape was to dream of riding across the prairie, the wind in her hair, crisp, clean air flowing around her. Things she'd taken for granted when she'd been free.

With the reassuring sound of the man's snoring, Peyton eased her way out of the tiny bedroom, her hand braced against the wall, her legs shaking. The bathroom door was closed and locked. When she pressed her ear to the thin door, all she could hear was the sound of retching.

The room spun with each step as she made her way through what should have been a living area. Windows had been covered with black trash bags held in place by duct tape. The only furniture in the space was a stained mattress in a corner. A man lay sprawled on his belly, half-on, half-off the mattress, his jeans partway down his thighs, passed out.

A wave of nausea and dizziness washed over Peyton. Her knees buckled. If she hadn't been bracing her hand against the wall, she would have fallen. She leaned into the paneling, pressing her cheek against the cold fake wood until the dizziness abated and her legs stopped shaking.

The urgency of her need to pee sent her staggering toward the door. As much as she didn't want to face Snake, she had no choice.

Once, one of the girls had urinated on one of the mattresses, unable to get up and use the only bathroom. As punishment, Snake had left her lying naked on the damp mattress all through a very cold Wyoming night. She'd almost died of hypothermia.

It wasn't until Snake and his men had decided to move the trailers that Peyton was able to help the girl off the mattress, clean her up and wrap her in a thread-bare blanket. She'd held her until her body had warmed and she'd quit shivering.

As soon as they'd parked the trailers, Snake had

his guys shoot the girls up with more drugs. Everything was a blur from there.

A blur was better than stark reality.

Peyton pushed the trailer door open. Cool air, blew against her exposed skin, making her shiver. She braced herself, expecting Snake to be standing there, ready to yell at her to get back inside.

He wasn't in his usual position when customers were with the girls.

Two men stood silhouetted in the glare of headlights several yards away from the trailer, their voices raised.

"That's fuckin' bullshit," a voice yelled.

"You pay to play." Peyton recognized Snake's hard tone and his usual sales pitch.

Desperate to relieve herself, Peyton descended the narrow steps, holding onto the handrail to keep from falling.

Once on solid ground, she hurried around the back of the trailer and into the woods before Snake ended his conversation, spotted her and stuck her with more drugs.

After she'd voided her bladder, she crept back toward the trailer and peered around. Though mind was still fuzzy and her balance uncertain, Peyton was more aware than she'd been in...hell...she didn't know how long.

The thought of escape skittered through her

foggy brain. With an angry man in his face, Snake's attention was otherwise occupied.

Peyton looked around for Snake's cohorts but didn't see them. She stepped backward, into the shadows of the nearby trees, closing one eye to get it adjusted to the dark while keeping the other eye fixed on what was going on in front of the trailer.

The two men still stood in front of the truck's headlights.

"It's half my paycheck," the heavier man said.

Snake shrugged. "Not my problem."

Barefoot and wearing only the big man's jacket, she wouldn't get far running into the woods. Especially since she didn't know where she was, or which way to go for help.

If she could stow away in the back of a customer's truck...

Hell. Timing was everything. Her brain wasn't functioning clearly enough. If Snake caught her trying to get away, he'd beat her to within an inch of her life—like he had the first time she'd tried to make a run for freedom.

"It wasn't that much last week," the man was saying.

Snake snorted. "Call it inflation. Now, if you're not gonna pay...leave."

The big man stepped closer to Snake. "I'm not leaving until I get what I came for."

Two other silhouettes joined Snake in the headlights.

"You heard the boss," a familiar voice said. "Leave."

Peyton eased around the clearing, careful not to make a sound, struggling to think straight when her mind and body were numb. She made it halfway around the clearing, having stopped within a couple of yards of a beat-up old pickup with several bales of hay piled in the back and no tailgate.

"Not leavin'," the big man said. "I came for the same services you sold me last week. I'm not going until I get it...at the *same* price."

Without a word, Snake lifted his chin.

The two men stepped toward the big man, then stopped short and held up their hands.

The big man held a handgun pointed toward them. "I ain't afraid of you. I'm here for the girls. Ain't leavin' until I've had me some."

Weak and shaking, her bare feet going numb with cold, Peyton shivered, afraid to move and draw attention to herself.

All at once, Snake lunged toward the big man. A flurry of motion ensued. A shot pierced the night.

All four men stood, frozen in place.

Then the big man slumped to the ground and lay still.

"Fuck." Snake bent over, retrieved the handgun

and straightened. "The bastard's even more trouble dead than alive."

The trailer door slammed open. The guy who'd been lying face down on the mattress in the living area poked his head out. "What the fuck's going on?"

"Not a goddamn thing." Snake faced the man. "Get your shit and get out."

The man in the doorway opened his mouth as if to say something, closed it and ducked back inside. He emerged moments later, carrying his shirt, his hand on his fly as he zipped his jeans. He strode toward the old truck close to where Peyton hid in the shadows.

The drunk who'd been in the room with Peyton emerged from the trailer. He'd pulled on his jeans and boots and carried his western-style shirt. "Where's my damn jacket," he demanded. He stumbled down the steps and staggered across the ground until he regained his balance, stopping short of the man lying on the ground behind Snake. "Holy shiiit. That man'sss dead."

"I don't know what you're talking about," Snake said. "I don't see a dead man." He turned to his guys. "Do you see a dead man?"

His two sidekicks shook their heads.

Snake turned back to the man standing in front of him. "Now, I suggest you get the hell out of here before we don't see you as well," he said in a low, dangerous tone.

The drunk backed away, his hands held high. "I don't want no trouble."

"Then, we're in agreement." Snake walked toward him, holding the gun he'd retrieved from the dead man. "Just to be clear...you didn't see anything. If word gets out about this little operation, we're not the only ones goin' down. How do you think your boss would feel about your extracurricular activities?"

The drunk shook his head. "I'd be fired."

Snake stepped closer. "And how would your old lady feel if she found out the money you spent didn't go toward a deer lease?"

"She'd divorce my assss."

"And take her family's money with her," Snake concluded, pressing the gun against the man's belly.

The drunk held up his hands. "I'm going. I'm going. I jusss want my jacket."

"Forget about it, Roy," the other man from the trailer called out. "Get in the truck."

"But..." The drunk frowned.

"Get your ass in the truck, Roy!" his buddy yelled.

"I'm coming," the drunk muttered. "Thisss iss shit, I tell ya." He staggered toward the truck, leaned on the hood as he rounded to the passenger side and finally climbed in.

Peyton waited until the drunk guy's buddy started the truck engine and switched on the headlights before she moved, figuring the lights would blind the others, and the engine would cover any noise she might make.

As the driver shifted into drive, Peyton stepped up on the rusty bumper and dove into the back of the pickup, landing between the loose bales of hay. She wedged herself deeper as the truck passed by the three men standing over the dead man.

Snake's voice carried over the roar of the pickup's engine, "Time to bug out."

Her heart pounding against her ribs, Peyton prayed they didn't notice she was missing until the truck carried her far enough away that they wouldn't find her.

Bumping across rutted roads shook Peyton's rattled brain, making her dizzy all over again. When they finally reached pavement, she closed her eyes, willing her pulse to return to normal and her thoughts to clear. Hopefully, the drugs would leave her system soon so that she could figure out her next step.

One thing was evident.

She'd escaped.

A fleeting pang of guilt swelled in her chest. Sure, she'd gotten out. But what about the other women who were still trapped in hell?

At last, the drugs, terror and effort it had taken to get away from Snake and the trailers took their toll. Though she fought hard to remain conscious, the steady rocking of the pickup lulled Peyton, and she succumbed to darkness.

WHAT SEEMED LIKE MOMENTS LATER, the truck rolled to a stop and bright lights shone down on the truck bed.

Peyton's eyes flew open. She stared up at the light, expecting them to be flashlights only to realize they were the kind of streetlights used in parking lots.

How long she'd been out, she didn't know.

The truck doors creaked open.

"I gotta have some coffee," the driver was saying. "You need some, too. Wouldn't do you any good to go home shit-faced drunk."

"I'm not sshhit-faced," Roy said as he slid out of the truck. "Fuck!"

"What the hell, Roy?" the driver said. Footsteps ground on gravel. "You can't even stand up."

Roy groaned. "Jusss tripped. I'm fine. Fuckin' fine."

"We have to get you sober enough you don't go shooting off your mouth," the driver said.

"Can't," Roy said. "Don't want to end up dead like that other guy."

"Shhh," the driver said. "You don't want anyone to overhear you."

"I'm shhushin'," Roy said. "Thanksss, Jim. You're a good friend."

"Yeah, whatever. Let's get that coffee," Jim muttered, his voice fading away.

"And sssomething to eat," Roy was saying.

Peyton's belly rumbled. How long had it been since she'd had anything to eat? The drugs had numbed everything, including her appetite. As they wore off, her stomach contracted. Food would be lovely.

She pushed that thought aside and waited a little longer before she raised her head out of the hay and looked over the sides of the truck bed.

The men had parked at a truck stop.

When Snake discovered she was missing and didn't find her around the trailer, he might come looking for Roy and Jim.

Peyton had to get out of the pickup before Snake or one of his thugs found it with her in the back.

She crawled to the open tailgate, looked right and then left before she slipped to the ground. Her legs buckled. Peyton fell to her knees. Using what little strength she could muster, she pushed to her feet and rounded the side of the truck, heading away from the buildings, passing between other vehicles, hunkering low. Soon, she reached the parking area where the tractor-trailer rigs and trucks pulling camp trailers were parked between diagonal lines.

All the trailers on the back of the big semis were secured with padlocks. She moved past the camp trailers, afraid that if they weren't locked, someone would be inside.

She thought about going into the truck stop and calling the state police but remembered Snake's threat and nixed the idea immediately. When she'd first tried to escape, he'd caught her and told her that if she went to the police, he'd be forced to kill the other women to keep them from talking and that he'd disappear before the police could find him. Then he'd come for her when she least expected.

No, she had to get help another way. But first, she had to get further away from the possibility of Snake finding her.

As she slipped around a large camp trailer, the sound of a horse whinnying drew her attention to a long, white horse trailer attached to a white truck with the logo printed on the sides of both the truck and trailer: Brighter Days Rehabilitation Ranch.

Something about the plaintive sound of the horse calling out and the name of the ranch called to Peyton. The rear door would be too heavy for her to maneuver without making her presence known. She rounded the back of the trailer to the other side where she found a narrow door. When she tried the handle, it didn't move.

Locked. She peered through the window into the darkness.

Again, the horse inside whinnied, the sound so sad it made Peyton's heart pinch hard in her chest.

She'd always loved horses and had ridden every chance she'd gotten...until she couldn't.

The horse inside the trailer pawed at the floor.

"Sounds like she's ready to be home," a female voice said from the other side of the big camper.

Peyton's heart leaped into her throat. Too late to run to the end of the trailer and hide, she dropped to the ground and rolled beneath the trailer.

CHAPTER 2

PEYTON LAY STILL, afraid to move. Lying on the ground, the cold sank into her bones, making her shiver. She wrapped her arms around herself, willing her body to be still. She couldn't be caught. Not now.

"It's been a long day for her," a male voice said getting closer to where Peyton lay beneath the trailer.

"Thankfully, it won't be much longer until we can tuck her into a warm stall with fresh hay and feed."

Two pairs of booted feet stopped in front of the narrow door, directly in front of where Peyton lay.

The metal-on-metal sound of a key being inserted into a lock was followed by the click of a latch, indicating the door was being opened.

The larger set of boots disappeared as the man entered the trailer, followed by the smaller boots.

"She seems to be holding up well," the man said.

"Yes, she is." The woman sighed. "Why are people

so cruel to animals? She deserves better than to be left to starve. Don't you, Lady?" the woman cooed. "We're going to get you fixed up in no time, and you'll live your best life from now on."

"Ready to get back on the road?" the man asked.

"Ready to be there," the woman replied.

They left the trailer, stepping down onto the pavement, and closed the door.

Peyton held her breath, listening for the sound of a key in the lock. When she didn't hear the metal scraping metal, hope bloomed.

The boots moved toward the truck. Doors opened.

Peyton rolled out from beneath the trailer enough to see a woman climbing up into the passenger seat.

"Want me to drive?" she asked.

Peyton pushed to her feet, grabbed the handle on the door and eased it open. Peyton waited until the woman started to close her door before she darted in and closed the trailer door behind her, hoping the sounds of closing doors were simultaneous. Once inside the trailer, she gasped.

The horse standing in the light shining through the small windows looked like a skeleton with hide stretched over its bones.

Tears welled in Peyton's eyes. "Oh, baby," she whispered. "You've had it even worse than I have."

As if the animal understood her words, she lifted her head and whinnied softly.

A truck's engine roared to life. A moment later, the trailer lurched beneath Peyton's feet. With only the jacket to keep her warm, she looked around and found a tack room with lead ropes, curry combs and two saddle blankets. She unfolded the blankets as wide as they would go and spread one across the mare's back. Then she sat on the floor of the trailer beside the horse and covered her bare legs with the blanket.

Soon, the steady rumble of the road beneath the trailer and the residual effects of the drugs lulled Peyton into a sleep plagued by nightmares.

Several times over the course of their journey, she woke shaking, her entire body trembling.

Each time, the mare bent her head and nuzzled her cheek as if telling her that everything would be okay. And each time, Peyton relaxed and fell back to sleep.

She had no way of tracking the amount of time that had passed.

When the trailer slowed to a stop, she jerked awake and blinked at the yellow light shining through the windows. Blinking back sleep, she pushed to her feet and peeked through one of the windows.

They'd parked in front of a barn.

Her heart pounding inside her chest, Peyton glanced around the confines of the horse trailer. These people with the horse might be good, or they might be bad. She still couldn't think clearly enough to trust anyone. Even if they were good people, they might think they were doing the right thing by contacting the local authorities.

Snake's threat echoed in her head. Peyton couldn't risk the lives of the other women. She had to find a way to help them without alerting law enforcement. She had to do it when she could think more clearly.

For now, she couldn't let anyone find her.

Peyton stroked the mare's nose. "You'll be okay," she said softly, praying she was right.

Then she slipped into the small tack room, draped the saddle blanket over a saddle tree and hid beneath it. Hopefully, the man and the woman wouldn't bother to look inside the tack room or lock the door once they led the mare out.

The muffled sound of footsteps sounded outside the trailer, and then a loud metal clank echoed inside, followed by the creak of hinges.

"Franklin and Vasquez wanted us to wake them when we got in," the woman was saying.

"No need," the man said. "We can get her settled in her stall without their help."

"Since she's shy of men," the woman said, "I'll lead her out if you could go and open up the barn and her stall."

"I can do that," the man said. "But I'd prefer you

wait to lead her out until I get back. Just in case she decides to bolt."

"Deal," the woman said.

One set of footsteps moved away from the trailer while the other set entered the back.

"Hey, Lady, we're finally home," she said, her tone soft and so soothing.

A lump lodged in Peyton's throat, and tears welled in her eyes.

Home.

Where was that? Her father had been killed in Iraq. Her mother had died of an overdose. The only relative she had left was her Aunt Rachel, and she was married to an alcoholic who'd resented Peyton's existence in their household.

She'd been working to save enough money to move off the reservation and maybe get a job in Missoula or Bozeman. In time, she'd wanted to go to college to be a nurse. She'd been taking online courses to complete her prerequisites.

"That's right," the woman half-talked, half-sang to the mare. "No one will hurt you here. You're safe."

Peyton swallowed a sob.

Safe.

If only.

"Okay," the man's voice said. "Barn and stall are open and ready for her."

At the sound of the male voice, Peyton stiffened, all the warm fuzzy feelings she'd experienced listening to the woman talking to the horse disappeared.

Deep down, she knew not all men were like the ones who'd abused her over the past few months. Still, she couldn't stop the gut reaction, the suspicion and distrust from welling inside and making her shake all over.

"We're just going to ease out of here, aren't we, Lady?" The woman spoke softly as she moved with the mare out of the trailer. Her voice faded as she led Lady away.

Peyton fought to slow her racing heart. Now was the time to get out of the trailer while the man and woman were busy settling the horse in the barn.

Tucking the horse blanket under her arm, Peyton slipped from the tack room and walked through the trailer, then stopped at the ramp, clinging to the shadows inside. She peered out into the night, studying the barnyard and searching for movement.

The sound of voices inside the barn reassured her that the man and woman were still occupied with settling the horse in her new home.

Peyton sucked in a deep breath and darted out of the trailer, heading for the side of the barn with the deepest shadows.

Once there, she sagged against the wall and slid to the ground.

The ranch house stood on a slight hill above the barn. A long low building stood a couple hundred feet from the barn. Based on the trucks parked outside the building, Peyton guessed it was where the single ranch hands were housed.

She shivered, determined to steer clear of it and the ranch hands, married and single. For that matter, she would do her best to steer clear of all men.

The man and the woman eventually exited the barn, closing the big barn doors behind them.

"Leave the truck and trailer. We can put it up tomorrow," the woman said. "I'm ready for a shower and bed."

"Me, too," he said and slipped his arm around her waist. "You're a good woman, Hannah. I swear you work miracles."

She smiled up at him in the light from the barn. "That's what we do here at Brighter Days...work miracles." She leaned up on her toes. "Have I told you lately that I love you?"

"Not since this morning," he said and pressed his lips to hers.

"I love you, Taz," she whispered against his mouth.

He wrapped both arms around her and pulled her close. "I love you more than you'll ever know."

"Mmmm," she moaned softly. "I like the sound of that."

He leaned back and stared down at her, a smile spreading across his lips. "Race you to the shower."

"You're on," she said and took off before he could say *Go*.

They ran, laughing all the way to the ranch house, disappearing inside.

Peyton remained in the shadows, her heart aching at the love she'd witnessed between Taz and Hannah. Was it real? Were they both in love or was one faking it? Would he break her heart someday by taking a lover or paying for sex?

After the lights blinked out in the upstairs room of the ranch house, Peyton shivered. A breeze kicked up. No matter how she tucked the horse blanket around her, she couldn't get warm enough. She couldn't stay outside for long. The nights got too cold. Add the windchill, and she'd die of hypothermia before morning. She was already sleepy. If she stayed where she was much longer, she'd drift off.

A whinny sounded from inside the barn.

Peyton knew without a doubt, that whinny was from the horse that had been in the trailer. She sounded scared and...lonely.

Like Peyton.

She pushed to her feet and moved to the edge of the shadows. Nothing moved. People and animals slept. Except for Peyton and Lady.

As quickly as her bare feet could carry her, Peyton ran to the smaller door at the front of the barn and prayed it wasn't locked.

When her hand turned the knob, it opened easily. She stepped across the threshold and out of the wind. For a moment she stood in the light shining in from the spotlight outside. She didn't dare turn on a light inside the barn. Someone might notice and come investigate.

The barn had a dozen stalls, a tack room to her right and stairs leading up into a loft. A small stack of hay filled the back left corner along with several large barrels Peyton assumed contained feed.

Lady whinnied as if sensing Peyton's presence, the sound emanating from a stall near the right rear of the barn.

The earthy scent of hay and horse manure soothed Peyton's soul. Once she committed the layout to memory, she closed the door behind her.

Peyton turned right. Holding her hand out in front of her, she walked forward until her fingers found the wall of the tack room. Running her hands along the wall, she passed the tack room, one stall, then the next, counting five before she stopped at the sixth.

A hoof pawed the ground on the other side of the gate.

"Hey," Peyton whispered, "it's me." She opened the stall door and slipped inside.

Lady touched her nose to Peyton's jacket.

Peyton stroked her gently. "Yeah, it's kind of scary in a new place. Especially when you don't know who to trust." She scratched behind the horse's ear. "You can trust me. I promise not to hurt you."

Peyton settled in the corner of the stall closest to

the door. Someone would have to come inside the stall to see her.

Out of the wind, and with the warmth of Lady standing nearby, Peyton tucked the blanket around her, drawing her legs up so they were completely covered. "I can stay for a little while," she said. "But I have to move by morning." She yawned, exhaustion pulling at her eyelids. "Get some rest."

Lady shuffled a few moments and then laid down in the wood chips lining the floor of the stall. She stretched out her neck and rested her head close to Peyton.

Peyton moved over and curled up beside the horse, drawing on her warmth, deeply sad at how bony the mare was.

Her last thought was that she was glad the horse had found a home. It gave her a tiny bit of hope for herself.

CHAPTER 3

"HEY, AUGUSTUS," Brody Franklin called out. "Could you toss me that pair of gloves?"

Augustus Walsh, the Fourth, shook his head. No matter how many times he'd reminded Franklin that he preferred to go by Gus, the man continued to address him by the name his father had written on his birth certificate application while his mother had slept off the effects of her painkillers. The document had been sent off to be recorded before she'd woken up and could do anything about it.

"What do you want with a pair?" Gus crossed to the shelf where extra pairs of leather work gloves were stored. "You only need one." He grabbed a pair and turned.

"Thanks for the reminder." Franklin shot him a middle finger from his left, and only, hand. "Vasquez will be here in a minute."

"Ah," Gus nodded. "Your right arm."

"Damn right, he is," Franklin said and chuckled at his own pun.

"Is Gus giving you shit again?" Xavier Vasquez entered the barn carrying a fifty-pound bag of feed on his right shoulder. He walked to the back of the building and dropped the sack on top of one of the covered buckets, then removed the lid on another. "No respect, I tell you." He ripped open the bag and poured it into the open feed storage container. "How long have you been here, Gus?"

"A month," Gus admitted.

"You should be completely in awe of our awesomeness by now," Franklin said.

Gus snorted. "I was until you planted a snake in my pillowcase."

Vasquez chuckled. "That was brilliant. Never saw a man scream like that or move that fast."

Franklin grinned and nodded. "Priceless."

Gus sighed. "I never should've admitted to my fear of snakes."

Franklin and Vasquez both nodded.

"Yeah." Vasquez's lips twisted. "That left you wide open."

"When I found that rat snake in the chicken coop..." Franklin lifted his shoulders and let them fall. "We had no other choice."

Gus's eyes narrowed. "Right." Since that moment, he'd checked every inch of his bunk, every night and slept with one eye open. He didn't trust these two pranksters. Yeah, both men were missing an arm, but that didn't slow them down. Not when there were jokes to be played on fellow veterans who were there to facilitate their recovery and reintegration into the civilian world.

To Gus, suffering the nightmares and anxiety attacks of PTSD had seemed minor and inconsequential compared to missing limbs.

However, Vasquez and Franklin's mental states were in a lot better condition than Gus's when he'd arrived at Brighter Days Rehab Ranch.

Thanks to Hannah and Taz Davila, the ranch hands and other veterans recuperating there, Gus's nightmares were becoming fewer and further between. He knew he needed to move on and rejoin his Brotherhood Protectors team in West Yellowstone. He needed to make space at the rehab ranch for others who needed help working through their issues.

Still...he hated to admit, but he was afraid of leaving the peace he'd found at Brighter Days. He was afraid that as soon as he left the ranch behind, the nightmares would return.

Franklin and Vasquez each manned one handle of a two-handled wheelbarrow full of soiled woodchips, hay and manure and rolled it out of the barn to dump it on the compost pile behind the barn.

The two worked together like two halves of a whole.

Movement out of the corner of Gus's eyes caught his attention. He turned toward the feed bins and the small haystack in the corner.

Had he imagined the shadow? Perhaps a raccoon had found its way into the barn and was scoping the feed bins for a potential late-night snack. Or a stray cat had found its way into the barn and hid amongst the hay bales. Either way, the animal needed to be caught and removed from the barn. It could carry rabies and be a danger to the other animals or ranch hands.

Gus was moving toward the feed and hay when a female voice sounded behind him.

"Ah, Gus. Just the man I wanted to see."

He turned to face Hannah Kendricks Davila, a beautiful sandy blonde who happened to be the backbone of Brighter Days Rehabilitation Ranch. Not only was she a hands-on rancher, but she was also a licensed therapist who helped the veterans and their horse rescues through some of their toughest mental and physical issues.

Gus had major respect and affection for this woman who'd helped him come to terms with one of the worst moments in his career as a Navy SEAL. She'd helped him realize that second-guessing his past actions wouldn't change the results. And she'd shown him that he could have a life worth living after leaving the military.

"Hannah," Gus said with a nod. "What can I do for you?"

She smiled. Her hands curled around a brown paper bag. "It's not what you can do for me, it's what you can do for yourself."

Here it was. The *talk* that would end his stay at the ranch and send him back out into the *real* world. He didn't respond, waiting for Hannah to continue.

"You already know what I'm going to say," she said softly.

He nodded.

"You've come a long way in the month you've been here. I like to think we've helped you, and it goes without saying that you've helped us a great deal. We couldn't have completely refenced the north pasture as quickly without your assistance."

"I should thank you for letting me be a part of that effort." Much of his recovery had a lot to do with the challenging physical labor he'd performed during his time there. Pounding T-posts into the ground, setting brace posts and stringing barbed wire had helped him work through his anger at the world and mostly his anger at himself for failing to save his teammate and best friend in the heat of battle. At the end of each day, he fell into his bunk too exhausted to dream.

"What if I said that I'd rather stay here at Brighter

Days than go back to work as a Brotherhood Protector?" he asked, his gaze on the stack of hay.

"As much as we appreciate all you've done in the past month," Hannah said, "we'd be doing you a disservice keeping you here when you have so much to offer your future clients. Our goal is to help *our* clients move on in life."

Gus frowned. "Then why do you keep Vasquez and Franklin from moving on?"

Hannah smiled softly, her gray-blue eyes shining in the sun. "Their enthusiasm for life is contagious. They're like poster boys for what it means to work together, and their comic relief is a morale boost for clients who've lost limbs and hope. I suspect they'll ultimately leave the ranch when they're ready to build homes and relationships. A bunkhouse isn't the place to do that." She smiled. "It won't be long before they find that special someone." She grimaced. "I'd much rather talk about you and your possibilities now that you're heading out on your own."

Gus's gut knotted. He rubbed his fist into his belly and gave her what he hoped was a confident smile. "What if the nightmares return?"

Hannah smiled. "You'll use the techniques we've practiced this month to control your anxiety or at least manage it until you can free yourself from whatever triggered the episode." She touched his arm. "And we're all just a phone call away. I'll answer calls, day or night, as will the others you've befriended during your stay."

Hannah had made this offer before. Hell, Vasquez and Franklin, despite their pranks, would help in a heartbeat.

Gus's only barrier to leaving the ranch was himself. It was time. He knew it. "How soon?"

"Tomorrow. Cookie's making your favorite for tonight's dinner."

"Sushi?" Gus said with a straight face.

Hannah's brow pinched. "No."

"Chicken cordon bleu?" He held back a grin as Hannah's frown deepened.

"No. I didn't know that was one of your favorites." She bit her bottom lip. "He's making a pot roast with carrots, potatoes and fresh-baked bread. Do you want me to ask him to change the menu?"

Gus chuckled. "No. Pot roast is perfect. I was just messing with you."

Her brow smoothed. "Good. He's got it in a slow cooker, and it smells amazing." She glanced down at the brown bag in her hands. "Which reminds me, I brought you some cookies. Oatmeal raisin." She handed him the bag. "Dinner is at the usual time. Six o'clock." She turned away and spun back a moment later. "Please understand. I'm not trying to get rid of you. If I thought you needed to stay longer, I'd keep you here."

"It's okay," Gus said. "I'll pack my stuff and leave

tomorrow morning. Stone texts me every other day, asking how I'm doing. I think it's his polite way of asking when I'll be back at work." He sighed. "Vacation's over."

Hannah snorted. "Some vacation. You've worked every day since you arrived."

"True." Gus stared out the door of the barn at the barnyard bathed in sunlight. "But it was different from anything I've ever done in the past. It never seemed like work."

One of Hannah's eyebrows rose. "Mucking stalls doesn't feel like work?"

Guys chuckled. "Okay, maybe mucking stalls is work. But it builds character."

"And women love a man who smells earthy," Vasquez said as he and Franklin reentered the barn, pushing the empty wheelbarrow.

"I seriously doubt they like the earthy scent of horse shit. Besides, what do you know about women?" Franklin demanded. "When was the last time you were on a date?"

"I've dated, in the past. Before…" He shrugged the shoulder of his missing arm. "It's not like there are a lot of single women here on the ranch or in Eagle Rock, for that matter."

Hannah's brow dipped. "There are a number of single women in the area. You just have to put yourself out there." She lifted her chin. "When was the last time you went to the Blue Moose Tavern in Eagle Rock?"

"Last Friday," Franklin answered. "The only single women I saw were waitresses, one of which was old enough to be my mother, maybe even my grandmother."

"Another was goth, all black hair and black fingernails," Vasquez said. "She looked like she boiled up men's balls for midnight snacks." He shook his head. "Nope. I like my balls just the way they are." He gave Hannah a sheepish grin. "No offense."

Hannah's eyes narrowed. "What we need is a community event with a dance to bring people together from all over the county. I'll work on that."

"You do that," Franklin said as he and Vasquez pushed the wheelbarrow past her and parked it in front of the third stall on the left. "In the meantime, we'll work on that earthy scent women love by mucking out more stalls."

Hannah shook her head, her attention returning to Gus. "They might not be as ready to leave as I thought," she murmured. "I'll work on that." She smiled. "See you at dinner?"

"Yes, ma'am," Gus responded and turned back toward the interior of the barn, trying to remember where he'd left off before Hannah had arrived.

Oh, yeah, the sound of movement near the feed bins.

Still carrying the sack of cookies Hannah had

given him, Gus walked to the bins, circled them and stared into the shadows made by the haystack.

Since Vasquez had already been there and had made enough noise to wake the dead pouring feed into a container, Gus doubted whatever had been lurking in the area had hung around. It had probably found its way out of the barn. He set the bag of cookies on the lid of one of the bins and shrugged off the jacket he'd worn when he'd come out to the barn that morning. After working for a while, he'd warmed up and didn't need it. He draped it over the bins next to the bag of cookies.

Though he had been given his marching orders, Gus didn't like leaving anything unfinished. He swung back to the stall he'd planned to work next and grabbed the shovel he'd leaned against the door.

Twenty minutes later, he had the stall cleaned of the soiled bedding, spread fresh woodchips down and filled the trough with water.

When he emerged from the stall, Franklin and Vasquez were wheeling another load of manure through the barn.

"That's the last one we have time for," Franklin said. "Vasquez and I are heading southeast to ride the fence and check for any damage from the winds we had last night. Want to come along?"

Gus shook his head. "No, thanks. I want to finish the remaining stalls. Then, I need to pack my gear."

The men stopped and set the back of the wheelbarrow down.

"Shipping out?" Vasquez asked.

Gus nodded. "About time I returned to West Yellowstone and got to work."

"Well, hell," Franklin said. "Just when we were getting used to having you around. I spotted a garter snake near the corner of the bunkhouse and hadn't had a chance to catch it."

A shiver rippled down the back of Gus's spine. Maybe leaving Brighter Days was a good thing. "Guess you'll have to terrorize the next resident who comes to stay."

"Guess so." Franklin frowned. "I don't suppose the Brotherhood Protectors could use a one-armed former grunt?"

Gus shrugged. "Never know until you ask. I'd start with Hank Patterson since it's his brainchild."

"He's been out here a couple of times," Vasquez said. "At the time, I didn't think we'd be of much use."

Gus raised an eyebrow. "And now?"

Vasquez shrugged. "Been working here long enough we can do everything anyone else can. We've even been training on handguns and rifles in our spare time."

"It's the damnedest thing." Franklin shook his head. "I shoot better lefthanded than I ever did righthanded. Although my penmanship still sucks."

"Don't wait for Hank to come to you," Gus

advised. "Reach out. What's the worst that could happen?"

"He could say no," Vasquez responded quietly.

"Then what?" Franklin sighed. "We can't muck stalls the rest of our lives."

Gus's chest tightened. "Have you thought about college? You have the GI bill, right?"

Vasquez nodded. "We've been doing online courses at night."

"We've finished all our core requirements and have started into our degrees," Franklin said. "I'm working on data security."

Vasquez grinned. "He's a wiz at hacking."

Franklin shrugged. "I figure you have to learn how to hack to know how to block hackers."

Gus grimaced. "I'm not sure I want to hear about your adventures in hacking."

"I haven't stolen bitcoins or sold government secrets," Franklin admitted.

Gus turned to Vasquez. "What about you? What are you working toward?"

Vasquez glanced away. "Game design. Like that's not a saturated field already."

Franklin bumped his shoulder into Vasquez. "Don't let him fool you. Games aren't all about the graphics. My boy, here, knows the logic and can anticipate what the user will choose next and how the villain should react. It's like he has a sixth sense."

"That and five bucks will get you a coffee."

Vasquez bent to grasp the handle on the wheelbarrow. "Come on, the day's not getting any younger, and it'll take time to get out to the southeastern fence line and back."

They left the barn, pushing the wheelbarrow between them.

Gus shoveled a few more stalls. Working his muscles always helped calm his mind and soothe his anxieties. Eventually, all the stalls were clean with fresh woodchips spread.

Gus closed the last stall he'd cleaned and hung his shovel and hay rake on the hooks lining the wall close to the tack room. He should be happy that this would be his last time mucking the stalls. He'd head back to West Yellowstone where Stone Jacobs probably had a client lined up who needed protection. It would be Gus's first assignment, working on his own. He'd helped as part of the team on other jobs, but none running solo.

His gut knotted as he walked along the bank of stalls, coaching himself to breathe in and out until the muscles in his belly relaxed. He stopped in front of the last stall and peered over the gate at the mare inside. Hannah had called their latest rescue Lady.

Her head hung low, appearing too big for a body so thin. Gus could count every bone. "Oh, Lady. You don't deserve this. Nobody deserves this kind of abuse."

He opened the stall door, stepped in and held out his hand.

She backed away and whinnied softly, her head swinging side to side.

Gus snatched his hand back. "Too soon? My apologies." He stepped out of the stall. "I wish I could be around to watch your recovery. You'll do well here at the Brighter Days. The people here will take good care of you." He closed the stall door, glanced around the barn one last time and sighed. It wasn't like he'd never return. The distance between Brighter Days Rehab Ranch and West Yellowstone wasn't that far. He could swing north every so often to check on everyone, including Lady.

He might as well go pack. If Cookie said dinner was at six, he expected people to show up on time and not smell like the inside of a barn.

Gus strode for the door, flipped the light switches off and stepped out into the barnyard.

The sun had sunk below the peaks of the surrounding mountains, plunging everything into a murky dusk. With the sun hiding behind the mountain, the temperature had already begun to drop.

When Gus turned to close the barn door behind him, a cool breeze brushed over the back of his neck.

"Shoot," he muttered. He'd left his jacket and the bag of cookies on the feed bins. Not so worried about the cookies, he didn't want to leave his jacket behind. His goal was to pack all his belongings that night for an early departure the following morning, jacket included.

He ducked back through the door. His hand was halfway to the light switches when he heard a scraping sound coming from the far left corner of the barn.

Lady whickered softly, the sound coming from her stall in the far right corner.

The hairs on the back of Gus's neck prickled.

CHAPTER 4

Gus flipped on the lights and glanced toward the feed bins at the back of the barn. A shadow shifted near the haystack.

Maybe it was a trick of his imagination. Gus hoped that was the case. He needed to get back to the ranch house, shower and shave before dinner. He certainly didn't have time to chase down a four-legged intruder, or worse...one with no legs.

God, he hated snakes.

He'd grab his jacket and the bag of cookies and hustle to the bunkhouse for that shower he so desperately needed. Since Vasquez and Franklin liked snakes so much, he'd leave it for them to deal with.

Gus strode the length of the barn, passing Lady's stall.

The emaciated horse whinnied softly.

"I know. I know," Gus whispered as if he was

striding through a library, rather than a one-hundred-year-old barn.

As he neared the feed bins, he frowned.

"I know I left my jacket and that bag of cookies here." He touched the top of the feed bin where he'd laid his jacket when he'd gotten too warm.

The jacket wasn't there. Nor was the bag of oatmeal cookies. His stomach rumbled. He should have eaten the cookies earlier. He loved Hannah's cookies.

Then a thought crossed his mind. Had Vasquez and Franklin returned from the southeast pasture and snuck in while Gus had been working? Were they up to pulling another prank on him?

Gus circled the line of feed bins. The jacket and the bag of cookies hadn't slipped off the lids of the bins onto the ground.

He expanded his search, his gaze sweeping over the ground further out from the bins until it landed on the haystack. Could he have moved the jacket off the bins and laid it on the hay and forgotten?

As he moved closer to the hay, he ruled out having laid the jacket on a bale. Nothing but hay was stacked in the corner.

A soft sound like that of crinkling paper came from the darkness behind the haystack.

Gus frowned, his first thought going to the shadow he thought he'd imagined. His next thought went to Franklin and Vasquez.

Slowly, he climbed the stack from a direction rarely accessed, based on the bales layered higher on that side. Placing his feet down slowly, carefully, he ascended until he reached the top layer.

This might be his only opportunity to catch Franklin and Vasquez in the act of pulling one last prank on him.

Without making a sound, he leaned over the edge of the stack.

As his head cleared the bale, he spied a saddle blanket draped over a figure, the bag of cookies and the sleeve of his black leather jacket.

Gotcha.

Not sure whether it was Franklin or Vasquez, Gus wondered where the man's sidekick was hiding. Apparently, not anywhere nearby or he would have warned his friend that Gus was hovering over him.

Gus dropped down onto the blanket, knocking over the person beneath. He landed on top of him, pinning him beneath the saddle blanket. "Ha! Thought you could pull one last prank—"

The figure beneath him bucked and squirmed. If he hadn't pinned the intruder beneath him, he'd have been kneed or violently kicked.

A high-pitched, feral snarl sounded through the thickness of the saddle blanket. Arms fought free of the blanket and small fists pummeled Gus's chest.

"What the—" Gus grabbed for narrow wrists and missed.

Fingernails scraped across his right cheek.

Gus cursed, captured a pair of wrists and pinned them with one of his own hands over his captive's head. Two hands ruled out Franklin and Vasquez.

"Who the hell..." With his free hand, he yanked the blanket aside.

Wide, dark eyes stared up at him. A mass of black, tangled hair spread across the blanket.

He stared down at a dirty face that most definitely belonged to a female.

"I'll be damned," he murmured. "Who the hell are you and what were you doing hiding behind the hay?"

Her gaze darted right and left all the while she strained to pull her wrists free of his grasp.

She reminded Gus of the raccoon they'd trapped in a cage a couple of weeks before. It had fought like a wildcat, hissing and scratching at the wire until its paws bled.

This woman had the same crazed look in her eyes. What bothered him most was that he'd put it there.

"Look," he said, "I'm not going to hurt you." He spoke slowly, softly, like he did when he wanted to calm a skittish horse. "I'm going to roll off you. You'll be free to go if you want. But know that if you're in trouble, maybe I can help."

He eased to his right, lifting his body off hers and

then pushed to his feet, his big frame effectively blocking her escape.

She fought free of the blanket and his coat and launched herself at the haystack. Her fingers dug into the hay, but she fell back. Again, she threw herself at the hay and fell, landing hard on her backside.

When she couldn't scale the stack, she backed herself into the corner, pulling bare legs up beneath her. She crouched, as if ready to dive past him if given a chance. The bulky brown jacket she wore swamped her body. She shoved the sleeves up her arms, freeing her hands.

Gus held up his hands and squatted so as not to intimidate her by his size. "I swear, I'm not going to hurt you. I'd let you run free, but you're clearly in no condition to brave the elements." He frowned. "Are you in trouble? Is there anyone I can call to help you?"

She shook her head.

"What about a family member?" he pressed.

Again, she shook her head.

"The sheriff?" he asked.

She shook her head faster.

He glanced at the blanket and the bag of cookies. "Are you hungry?"

Her eyes widened in her gaunt face. She looked like a starving stray cat, hungry but afraid to trust anyone.

"At least let me get you some clothes and some food. You look like you haven't eaten in days."

She didn't respond, her gaze fixed on him.

"What's your name?" he asked.

Nothing.

Like Lady, she'd backed herself into a corner, afraid, not able to trust anyone.

In this case, Gus couldn't leave her in a stall and work on that trust issue over time. If he backed out of the narrow space, he was certain she'd run. If she did, where would she go? It was getting dark. Temperatures got cold at night. She wasn't wearing shoes or anything covering her legs. Hell, she'd die of hyperthermia before morning, if the wolves or bears didn't find her first.

"Please," he said. "Let me take you up to the ranch house. I'm sure Hannah has some clothes you could wear and maybe some shoes in your size."

As her head moved side to side, a shiver shook her body. She wrapped her arms around herself as the shaking continued. Her knees dropped to the ground, and she fell forward onto her hands.

Gus stepped toward her.

The woman rose on her haunches and threw herself past his legs, stumbled, rolled and got up on all fours.

Gus spun. "Wait!"

Instead of racing for the barn door, she crawled to Lady's stall, pulled herself up high enough to unlatch the gate and fell through the opening, catching Lady around the neck.

Lady uttered a startled nicker but didn't shy away. She stood still while the woman leaned heavily against her and then slowly slid to her hands and knees.

"Please," she whispered, "don't hurt me."

He stopped short of where she swayed on all fours. "Let me help you," he begged.

She trembled so violently she dropped onto her side and curled into the fetal position, her teeth chattering.

When Gus moved forward this time, she didn't protest. She couldn't. Her eyes rolled back, and her entire body went from rigid and shaking, to completely limp.

Gus slid his arms beneath her back and legs. He lifted her into his arms, backed out of the stall and kicked the gate shut.

She weighed nothing.

Gus was shocked at how light she was in his arms.

He strode through the barn and out the door, desperate to get this woman help, afraid he might already be too late.

No. No. No.

He couldn't be too late. Not this time. This wasn't Afghanistan. The person in his arms wasn't his best friend and fellow Navy SEAL. The woman in his arms hadn't stepped on an IED.

His heart raced, pounding so hard that he felt like he was having a heart attack. "No," he said softly to himself as he crossed the barnyard. "It's just a panic attack. Your heart is fine. Just breathe."

He stopped for a moment and lifted her face close to his. For a moment, he held his breath, willing his pulse to slow, his heart to quit beating so hard and fast, long enough for him to hear or feel...

Warm air from her nose brushed across his cheek.

Gus let go of the breath he'd been holding and continued toward the ranch house.

As he climbed the porch steps, he called out, "Hannah, Taz, anyone! Help!"

He fumbled with the doorknob, trying not to jostle the woman in his arms.

Footsteps sounded, running toward the door.

Taz yanked open the door. "What the—" Immediately, he stepped back and shouted over his shoulder. "Make way."

Half the residents of the rehab ranch stood around their eyes wide.

Hannah waved Gus forward. "Bring her into the great room and lay her on the couch." She led the way, calling over her shoulder, "Someone call 911."

"I will." Vasquez pulled out his cell phone.

"Do that," Gus said, "but I'd feel better if we met the ambulance on the way to Eagle Rock."

"Gotcha." Vasquez stepped back as he called the emergency number.

"I'll drive," Taz said. "We can take the Denali."

"Before you load her up, let me get some blankets." Hannah darted out of the great room.

Gus still held the woman in his arms, not ready to let go of his burden.

"Where did you find her?" Taz asked.

"In the barn," Gus said, staring down at the woman's face, willing her eyes to open. "I think she was hiding behind the bales of hay the entire time we were mucking stalls. I thought I heard something when Hannah came out earlier but didn't check it out until right before I was ready to come in and clean up for dinner." He shook his head. "Had I known she was there, I could've done something earlier."

Taz stared at the woman in Gus's arms. "How *did* you find her?"

Gus told him how he'd forgotten his jacket and gone back inside to retrieve it. He shot a glance toward Vasquez and Franklin. "I thought you two were pranking me, hiding behind the haystack to jump out with a snake or something." He frowned down at the woman. "I came up over the top of the stack and dropped down on what I thought was one of you two hiding under a horse blanket."

"Damn," Franklin said. "That had to hurt."

Gus nodded. "I didn't know who I had until I pulled the blanket away from her face. I still had her pinned. She fought like mad to get free."

"Is that what happened to your face?" Hannah

reentered the great room with her arms full of blankets.

"Yeah," Gus had forgotten the scratches. "Not long after she started shaking, she ducked past me into Lady's stall and passed out."

"She's obviously been traumatized by something or someone." She dropped the stack of blankets on one of the chairs, took one off the top and spread it across the couch. "Lay her on this one," she directed. "It'll be warm and soft against her skin. We can wrap her in it and take the others out to the SUV." She turned to the other men standing in the room. "The rest of you can leave. Give her some privacy."

Taz nodded and herded the men out. "I'll go warm up the Denali."

Gus waited until the room cleared before he laid the woman on the blanket.

"Sweet Jesus," Hannah murmured. "She's naked except for the coat. I'd remove it, but it's probably the only thing that's kept her alive. She looks like she's been on the run for a while. Did she happen to tell you her name?"

"I asked," he said. "She wasn't talking, until just before she passed out."

Hannah tucked the blanket around the stranger and straightened. "What did she say then?"

His gut knotted. "Please, don't hurt me."

"Someone did this to her. We should notify the sheriff."

Gus shook his head. "I asked her if she had family I should call. She shook her head. When I asked if I should call the sheriff, she shook her head even more. I get the feeling she doesn't want to involve the law."

Hannah's brow furrowed. "She might have been raped. Whoever did this needs to be caught before he does it to someone else."

"I agree," Gus said, his hands bunching into fists. "But until we get her to talk, I'd rather respect her wishes. If we report her situation to law enforcement, it becomes public record."

Hannah lifted one of the woman's hands. "When the healthcare workers see this, they're going to have to report it." She pointed to the bruises around the unconscious woman's wrist.

The anger that had been simmering inside Gus burned hot. The woman had been restrained naked, most likely raped and practically starved.

"Whatever happens, she needs protection until the bastard is caught." Hannah met Gus's gaze. "We need to call the sheriff."

Gus shook his head. "Let me call Stone Jacobs."

Hannah's eyebrow rose. "Your boss?"

"Yes, ma'am."

"And get the Brotherhood Protectors involved?" Her lips curled upward. "Good. I'd feel better knowing someone is looking out for her. Why don't you call Hank Patterson? He's closer."

"I know." Gus bent to gather the woman into his

arms. "I'll let Jacobs make that connection *after* he assigns me to this mission."

Hannah gathered the other blankets. "I'm happy you'll be rejoining your team. And even happier that you've found your first assignment."

Gus carried the stranger out of the ranch house to the waiting Denali, hoping his *mission* didn't die before they got her to the hospital.

CHAPTER 5

PEYTON SWAM in and out of consciousness, viewing the world like disconnected scenes in a movie that made no sense. She was too tired to resist when someone lifted her into the back seat of a vehicle. Warm blankets were wrapped around her. She blinked her eyes open and looked up into a man's face with eyes so blue they reminded her of the summer sky on the reservation.

She tensed but didn't have the strength to fight or run.

He looked down at her and smiled, gently stroking her hair back from her forehead.

Peyton flinched when he raised his hand again.

His brow puckered, and his hand dropped to his side. "Too soon?" He nodded. "It's okay. You're going to be okay. I won't let anyone hurt you." He spoke in a tone as soft and warm as the blankets she was cocooned inside.

Because she had no other choice, she believed him and let sleep claim her. If it was a dream, at least she'd feel safe until she woke.

The next time she opened her eyes, she was being lifted onto a stretcher and transferred into the back of an ambulance.

In the fog of her mind, all she could think was if she lived, they died. She couldn't go to a hospital. They'd find her.

"No," she whispered. "They can't know."

"It's okay." Again, that warm, soft voice sounded next to her ear. She looked up.

The man with the blue eyes looked down at her. "I won't let anyone hurt you."

Peyton tried to sit up. A strap over her chest kept her from rising. She tried to raise her hand, but it was pinned to her side. "Not...just...me."

"What did she say?" another voice asked.

Blue Eyes leaned close. "Do you need something?"

"Need...to...be...dead," she said, her voice hoarse, barely above a whisper.

"I can't let you die," Blue Eyes said. "But I will make sure no one hurts you again. I promise."

She turned her head from side to side. He didn't understand. If she lived, they died. She tried again to sit up. "Please."

"I'm giving her something to calm her," the other voice said.

Seconds later, her vision faded to black.

PEYTON'S EYES opened to light so bright she thought she might have died and gone to the heaven her mother had prayed to every night when she'd been a little girl.

Nearby voices brought her back to Earth.

"The doctor examined her," a woman's voice said. "As you suspected, she's been raped. Probably more than once. We've administered the rape kit and, hopefully, gathered semen samples. Based on the bruises all over her body, she's been forcibly restrained, battered and abused. Needle marks indicate drugs have been administered. Whether she took them willingly or not, we won't know until she wakes and tells us. Why wouldn't she want us to report this?"

Peyton's eyes burned, and a single tear slipped from one corner, running down the side of her face into her ear.

The woman was talking about her.

"We appreciate your concern, Nurse Foster," another female voice reasoned. "When she was awake, she expressed her desire not to go to the police. It's her choice as to whether the rape is reported. We won't know what she wants until she wakes again."

Peyton closed her eyes. They'd expect answers she wasn't ready to give. She needed to think. As hard as she tried to concentrate, she couldn't form coherent thoughts.

"Okay." The nurse sighed. "We'll wait until she wakes."

Good. Peyton would pretend to be asleep until she could come up with a plan."

"And once she's conscious," Nurse Foster continued, "she can tell us who she is and who did this to her. It's scary to think bastards like that are free to do this to women."

"I want him caught as badly as you do," the other woman said. "Look, my name is Hannah Davila. Here's my card. Call me when she wakes. Since we found her on the ranch, we need to know how she got there and who might be after her. For all we know, our guests could be in danger."

"Fair enough," the nurse said. "And until she wakes, we can't allow any men into her room. Especially the one who brought her in. She'll have to clear him personally when she comes to."

"Understood," the one called Hannah said. "In the meantime, he'll stand guard outside her door. Not only is he a trained bodyguard, he's prior military and a Navy SEAL."

"And I'll bet our patient is the one who scratched his face." The nurse's tone was flat.

"She did," Hannah said. "He caught her as an intruder in our barn. She's so traumatized she fought to get away before he could release her. But he didn't tie her up, bruise or rape her. He's a good man who has sacrificed so much for our country."

"I've seen what some of our military men can do to women," Nurse Foster said. "He's not allowed in the room. I'll have security park outside her room to make sure."

"Good," Hannah said. "Then we can be doubly sure no one hurts her again."

"I have rounds," the nurse said. "I'll be back to check on our patient in an hour. Visiting hours are over. If you're not family, you'll have to leave."

"I'm leaving," Hannah said. "Let me check on our charge once more."

Keeping her eyes closed, Peyton listened for the sound of footsteps. She didn't hear any but sensed someone standing by her bed.

"Hey, sweetie," Hannah's voice sounded beside Peyton. "I don't know who you are or what you're running from, but we're going to do our best to help you. Gus will be outside your room the entire time you're here in the hospital. He's here to protect you, not hurt you. I know it must be hard to trust anyone after what you've been through, but he's one of the good guys. I'll be back. I hope you feel better soon. And when they let you loose from the hospital, you're welcome to stay at Brighter Days. We specialize in helping people reclaim their lives after suffering as much as you have."

Long, slender fingers wrapped around hers and squeezed gently. "And Cookie makes the best sweet potato pie. You might want to stay with us just to taste his cooking. Sleep well. I'll see you soon."

Hannah released her hand.

Peyton counted to five in her head before she peeked beneath her lashes at the woman walking toward the door.

She had long, sandy-blond hair pulled back in a low ponytail. Tall, athletic and wearing jeans and a blue chambray shirt, she looked like someone Peyton could be friends with...in another life.

Her current life wasn't anything she'd wish on anyone. Now that she'd lived it, she didn't feel like she belonged anywhere. Certainly, not back on the rez. When people found out what she'd been forced to endure, they'd look at her like she felt...like she was dirty...filthy...untouchable. No one would want her around. She didn't want to be around and would end her own life to escape the horror.

But she couldn't.

Yet.

Not until she freed the other girls who'd been stolen from their homes and communities and forced into sexual servitude.

Her stomach heaved at the images roiling in her head. The countless faces of men who'd come through the trailer, of hands on her body, pinching, squeezing, hitting.

All she wanted was to die.

No.

Peyton forced back the overwhelming hopelessness that threatened to consume her. She had to free the others. To do that, she couldn't let them know she was alive. First, she had to get strong enough to find them and somehow free them from the bastards running the trailer operation.

Though she tried to stay awake, the gray fog of sleep claimed her.

SHE WAS FLYING *across the prairie riding bareback on Little Joe, Matt White Feather's paint pony. Since he was working different hours at the same convenience store where Peyton worked and going to community college part-time, he had little time to ride the horse, and he let her ride whenever she wanted. He'd even offered his saddle.*

Peyton preferred to ride bareback. She was closer to the horse and felt as if she could feel his thoughts, and he could sense hers. With the slightest pressure from her thighs, he would change directions, slow, stop or race like the wind.

She lifted her face to the sky and breathed in the cool Wyoming air.

Little Joe sped up.

Peyton brought her attention back to the land in front of her. The horse headed straight for a stand of trees, going faster and faster. No matter how hard she squeezed her legs around him, he wouldn't slow.

Without a saddle horn to hold onto or reins to pull back, she could do nothing but hang onto a handful of his dark main.

Little Joe plunged into the trees, dodging left and right.

Peyton slid side to side with each change in direction. Just when she thought she would fall off, they emerged into a clearing.

Little Joe came to a sudden stop and reared high into the air.

Peyton slid off his back and landed hard on the ground, the wind knocked from her lungs.

Little Joe galloped away.

She fought to drag in a breath to call him back. When she finally got her lungs to work, she gulped in air and slowly sat up.

Her heart sank into the pit of her belly as a scream rose in her throat.

Three dirty camp trailers stood in front of her.

Snake and his two sidekicks were headed toward her.

"It's a good thing you came back," Snake said. "I was just about to kill the others."

Peyton scrambled to her feet, spun and ran back toward the trees.

She hadn't gone three feet before arms wrapped around her and yanked her off her feet.

Peyton screamed and fought to get away.

"Shh," a warm, deep voice breathed into her ear. "It's okay. You're safe. Shhh."

The more the voice sounded in her head, the slower she moved until she stood still, held in arms that didn't squeeze the life out of her, against a solid body that wasn't holding her down, forcing her to do things she didn't want to do.

"Wake up, Sweet Lady Jane," the voice said. "You're safe. I'd let you go, but I'm afraid you'll fall. Can you stand?"

Her bare feet were on the floor. Surely, she could stand. Peyton nodded.

The arms loosened around her.

Her legs wobble like a newborn colt. Without him holding her up, they buckled. If his arms hadn't immediately wrapped around her again, she would have hit the floor.

"Let me help you back into the bed," the man with the voice that soothed said.

Before she could protest, he scooped her up and laid her across the sheets. Only then did her gaze connect with eyes so blue they reminded Peyton of... "Wyoming sky."

He straightened, his lips twisting into a wry smile. "Wyoming sky? I don't understand."

Door hinges squeaked, and a man shouted, "Dude! Step away from the patient!"

Blue Eyes raised his hands and backed away from the bed with a wink. "I'm backing away."

"Ma'am, are you okay?" A man in a hospital security uniform stepped between Blue Eyes and Peyton.

She nodded. "I'm fine," she croaked.

"Is this man bothering you?" the guard asked.

Was he? Peyton's brow pinched. Her answer didn't seem to require a clear mind or any thought. "No."

"What was he doing in your room?" the guard asked.

Peyton looked around the guard, her gaze connecting with Blue Eyes. "He saved me."

The man was a stranger. Other than landing on top of her and scaring the shit out of her, he hadn't tried to hurt her like all the others. And he'd saved her from Snake.

She frowned. Or had that been a dream?

A woman in blue scrubs rushed into the room. "What's going on?" Her gaze landed on Peyton. "You're awake." Her glance shifted from Peyton to the guard and then to Blue Eyes. "I thought I told you to keep this man out of our patient's room."

The guard glared at Blue Eyes. "He'd gone to the break room. I ran to the men's room. I was on my way back when I heard the patient screaming. I found him in here with her."

The nurse pointed to the door, her eyes narrowing at Blue Eyes. "Out! Now! Before I call the police."

Blue Eyes backed toward the door. "She was alone

and screaming. I promised I wouldn't let anyone hurt her."

The nurse pulled a cell phone from her pocket. "I'm calling the police."

"No," Peyton called out, her voice barely a whisper. She tried again. "No. He can stay. He's...one of the...good guys." As she said the words, she wasn't sure she believed them. Was there such a thing as good guys?

Could she ever learn to trust a man again?

Though her head said, *No, don't trust any man,* deep in her heart, she knew...this man could be the exception.

Still, she'd keep her eyes open. As soon as she could get around on her own, she'd get a knife, pepper spray and a gun. And she'd take self-defense lessons.

After she managed to free the others, and if she decided to stay in this world, she refused to ever be a victim again.

The nurse crossed her arms over her chest. "Only family members are allowed to stay past visiting hours. I'm afraid he can't stay."

"I'm her bodyguard," Gus said. "It's my job to protect her."

The nurse looked from Gus back to Peyton. "Is that so?"

Peyton met Gus's blue-eyed gaze and nodded slowly.

Nurse Foster's chin lifted. "If that's the case, what's her name, and why didn't you tell me earlier?"

Gus's gaze remained connected to Peyton's. She gave him an almost imperceptible shake of her head.

The nurse had asked Gus the question. Even if she'd directed the question to Peyton, Peyton wouldn't have answered and risked her name showing up on some database. If Snake was looking for her, he might think to check all the hospitals looking for Peyton Running Bear.

Gus's eyebrow cocked, and he shifted his gaze to Nurse Foster. "Her name is Jane."

The nurse rolled her eyes. "Next, you'll tell me her last name is Doe."

Gus shook his head. "No, of course not. It's Jane Black. I didn't tell you earlier because we didn't want her name to appear on any databases. If her attacker is looking for her, he might think to call the hospitals and ask for Jane Black."

Nurse Foster's eyes remained narrowed for a moment longer. "I need you to step out of the room, Mr..."

"Walsh," the man said. "Gus Walsh. You can call me Gus."

"Mr. Walsh, please step out of the room for a moment. I need to get Miss Black's vital signs."

Gus met Peyton's gaze.

She nodded.

"I'll be right outside the door." Gus turned to the security guard.

The guard shot a glance toward Nurse Foster.

"You, too," she said.

The two men left the room. The door swung closed.

Nurse Foster then turned to Peyton. "Is your name Jane Black?"

Peyton had never felt comfortable lying. But too many lives depended on her retaining her anonymity. Without hesitation, she answered, "Yes."

"Is that man really Gus Walsh?" the nurse continued.

Whether he was or not, he'd introduced himself to Nurse Foster as Gus Walsh. Peyton nodded. "Yes."

She lowered her voice and took Peyton's hand. "Is he the one who hurt you?" The nurse stared into her eyes; her brow puckered, concern etched deeply into the lines across her forehead.

Tears filled Peyton's eyes. "No, he's trying to help me."

"Why did you scratch his face."

The tears slipped from the corners of her eyes. "I didn't know he was trying to help me. I thought...I thought he was going to..." She looked away, shame burning intensely in her chest. "But he didn't. He's trying to help me." She squeezed the nurse's hand. "Please, let him stay. He makes me feel...safe."

Nurse Foster held tightly to Peyton's hand,

staring into her eyes. "He didn't threaten you to make you say that?"

Peyton gave the nurse a hint of a smile. "No. I truly believe that he and Hannah are trying to help me. I can't let the people who did this to me find me. They can't know I'm alive. I need them to think I'm dead until we can find them and bring them to justice."

The nurse's eyes widened. "Them? There was more than one man?"

Peyton nodded, closing her eyes. Done with the questions and so very tired. "How soon can I leave the hospital?" she asked.

"I imagine when you're strong enough to walk out. The doctor will decide. You need to get your strength up. You're malnourished. We have you on an IV to get some nutrients into your body. But that's not good enough. You need to eat to fuel your body and rebuild muscle mass."

Peyton couldn't wait too long. Snake might decide her disappearance would be too risky, especially when he couldn't find her body.

"So, I need to eat?" she asked without opening her eyes.

"Yes, ma'am." The nurse's fingers clicked across a keyboard as she noted Peyton's blood pressure and pulse. Then she shined a light into her eyes. "It's late, but they have someone on duty in the hospital kitchen twenty-four-seven. Do you want me to have something sent up? The doctor doesn't have you on any dietary restrictions, just a cautionary note to take it slow."

Peyton opened her eyes. "Could I get a hamburger and French fries?" Peyton asked.

"Absolutely," the nurse responded with a smile.

"And can I get one for my bodyguard? I think I made him miss dinner."

"I can do that." The nurse frowned again. "Know that if anyone is pressuring you to say or do anything against your will, I'm here. I'll help you in any way I can."

"Thank you, Nurse Foster." Peyton's heart swelled at the woman's offer.

"I have a daughter in college. I live in constant fear for her. Even more so now." She glanced at Peyton's wrists and the purple bruises ringing them. "No man has the right to abuse a woman."

"Tell your daughter that if she gets a flat tire on a deserted highway, not to accept a ride from anyone. Drive that flat tire and ruin the rims if she has to. Just don't accept a ride or walk. She should limp back to a town on the flat, park in a well-lighted area and use her cell phone to call for a tow truck."

The nurse studied Peyton for a long moment and finally nodded. "I'll tell her. Now, get some rest. I'll have food delivered within the hour."

"Thank you," Peyton said, letting her eyelids drift downward. "If you can't let...Gus...in my room, could you leave the door open? I get anxious when he's out of sight."

"Of course. And if you're comfortable with him, he can come into your room. The lounge chair in the corner reclines. His feet might dangle off the end, but at least he could stretch out and get a little sleep."

Peyton smiled at the image in her mind of Gus on the lounge chair, his feet hanging way over the footrest. "I'll let him know."

"Remember," Nurse Foster said, "if you need something or want to talk, I'll be here until six o'clock in the morning. I'll also leave you my personal cell phone number if you need to talk after I leave the hospital."

"Thank you." She managed to open her eyes long enough to smile at the older woman. "It means a lot to me to know I have backup."

Nurse Foster left the room, propping the door open behind her.

Peyton watched her leave. As she passed through the door, Gus joined her.

The nurse leaned close to Gus and talked for several long minutes. Finally, she nodded, turned and disappeared out of the doorway.

The weight of Peyton's eyelids dragged them downward again. "Why am I so tired?"

"You've been through a lot." His deep, warm voice washed over her like melted chocolate, eagerly finding every nook and cranny of her body to invade.

Once the nurse was gone, Gus entered Peyton's room. "Do you mind if I rinse the blood off my face? It's making the staff crazy."

"I'm not saying I'm sorry," she murmured.

"I'm not asking you to." He turned toward the sink in the corner.

Peyton kept her eyes half-closed, studying the man from beneath her lashes.

Gus bent over the sink in a corner of the room and scrubbed the crusted blood from his cheek. When he was done, he dried off and sank into the lounge chair.

When Gus put the leg rest up, Peyton smothered a giggle.

Gus nodded toward his feet, hanging six inches over the end of the footrest. "This chair was made for short people."

"The window seats have cushions," Peyton suggested.

"I'll make do with the lounger," he assured her. "You should rest."

"I will," she said. "Soon."

A knock sounded on the doorframe. "Did someone ask for a hamburger and French fries?" A man dressed in white coveralls appeared in the doorway, pushing a cart that smelled so good that Peyton's stomach rumbled and her mouth watered. "I did," she said.

The man pushing the cart grabbed one of the

covered dishes, crossed the room and laid the plate on the rolling table. He pushed the table over to the bed and raised Peyton's head until she was almost sitting up straight. "Better?"

Other than being a little light-headed, she did feel better. "Yes. Thank you."

The food delivery guy returned to his cart and lifted another covered plate, handing it to a surprised Gus. "Bon appétit," he said and disappeared.

Gus's brow twisted, and his lips pressed into a thin line as he stared down at the plate. "What's this?"

"A burger." Peyton fumbled with the fork and knife, trying to cut her burger in half. "It's not your favorite pot roast whipped up by the ranch cook, but it's all I could request in a pinch."

Gus lifted the lid off his plate and stared down at the burger. "It looks amazing. I didn't realize I was hungry until I smelled the food on the cart."

Peyton nodded, pressing the knife through the bun and burger, effectively cleaving it in two. Her hands fumbled with the half she attempted to pick up. The contents within the bun threatened to slide out one side. After she shoved it back together, she took a bite and moaned.

"Is that a good moan or a bad moan?" Gus asked.

"Oh, so good," she said around the bite of food in her mouth. Chewing slowly, she savored the morsel and several more.

Gus ate in silence, finishing his burger well before

Peyton. He lifted a fry, dipped it into catsup and paused with the fry halfway to his mouth. "I promised you that I wouldn't let anyone hurt you again. To effectively keep that promise, I need to know more about you, the situation and the people involved."

Peyton had just taken a bite out of her burger when Gus posed the request.

She chewed thoughtfully, glad for a few extra seconds to decide what she could tell him and what she would keep to herself.

Finally, she swallowed and looked into Gus's eyes. She didn't want to tell anyone about what had happened to her. It was all...humiliating, disgusting and made her sick to her stomach.

He leaned forward, lowering the leg rest. "Look, if you don't feel comfortable talking to me, maybe you'd feel better talking to a female. Hannah will be back soon. What you need to remember is that you didn't ask to be abused. None of it was your fault. You have nothing to be ashamed of."

He reached for her hand.

Peyton automatically flinched, drawing as far away as she could from his touch.

"Sorry." He brought his hand back to his side. "I only want to help."

"You can help me best by getting me out of here," she said. "Sooner rather than later."

CHAPTER 6

GUS WAS STUMPED. If his client wouldn't talk to him, he couldn't anticipate trouble effectively. He couldn't blame her. After what she'd been through, he doubted she'd feel like sharing the horrible details.

He'd notified Hannah when he'd been out in the hallway while the nurse had taken Jane's vitals.

Jane.

He knew it wasn't her name. She'd said she needed to be dead, that the people who'd held her couldn't find her.

Why?

He was there to protect her. He wouldn't let them past him.

"Okay. We'll work on getting you out of here. But you're in no shape to go off on your own. You wouldn't get too far before you passed out. You need time to recover and rebuild your strength."

She shook her head. "I don't have time."

"You can't fight these people if you don't have the strength to walk across the room."

She lifted her chin. "I made it to the barn."

"From where?" he asked.

Her brow furrowed. "I don't know."

"How did you get to the barn?"

"In a horse trailer," she said.

Finally, they were getting somewhere. "The one they brought Lady home in?"

She nodded. "She called to me."

"What do you mean?"

"I think she knew I was there and needed help." Jane looked down at her hands. "I know it sounds ridiculous, but I might not have gotten into that trailer if not for Lady."

"I'm glad you did. And I'm glad I found you behind that haystack before morning. It gets cold at night, even in the barn. You could've died from exposure. As it is, I don't know how you made as far as you did with only a coat to keep you warm."

She looked toward the window. "I didn't have a choice. I couldn't die."

"Why do you say that?"

Her lips pressed together. "I need you to get me out of here."

"We'll work on that."

"No," she met his gaze and held it. "You don't understand. I need to go now." She flung back the blanket covering her legs and reached for the IV in her arm.

Gus leaped to his feet. "Don't—" When he reached out to cover her hand with his, she jerked back, her eyes wide, her body stiff.

He didn't back away this time and kept his hand over hers on her arm. "Leave the IV in until we clear you with the doctor."

The door swung open, drawing their attention.

Hannah entered, followed by Nurse Foster. "Oh, good. I'm glad she's awake." She hurried over to Jane's bedside and smiled down at her. "Hey." Then her gaze shifted to where Gus held his hand over Jane's on her IV. "Is there a problem?"

Gus released his hold on Jane's hand and backed away. "She wants to leave."

Hannah frowned. "You're not well enough."

"I have to go. Too much time has passed. It might be too late already." Jane swung her legs over the side of the bed and pushed herself to her feet.

Gus was there to catch her when she fell.

He wrapped his arms around her as she leaned into his chest.

"What's wrong with me?" she said against his shirt as she began to shake.

"You're weak," Hannah said. "And probably coming down from the drugs you've been given."

"I can't stay here," she said, tears slipping from her eyes. "If they find me—"

"They won't find you tonight," Hannah said. "At least give yourself until the morning. We'll arrange transport to get you back out to Brighter Days, where you'll be safe and have time to recover."

"I have to leave," Jane said, her teeth chattering, her body trembling against Gus.

His heart hurt for her. He wished he could do more to help her.

Nurse Foster stepped around them and slipped a syringe into the IV line. "I'm giving her something the doctor prescribed to calm her. She needs sleep and a chance for the nutrients and antibiotics to work."

"No." Jane shook her head and then went limp in Gus's arms.

He lifted her and gently laid her in the bed, drawing the sheet and blanket up over her bruised legs and body.

She lay so still, her chest barely rising with each breath.

"She's terrified," Hannah said. "We can't keep knocking her out when she gets upset. We'd be no better than the people who kept her drugged during her captivity."

"She can't leave on her own," Gus pointed out.

"No, but she's afraid they'll find her if she stays here." Hannah met the nurse's gaze. "As long as her vital signs are stable, she might be better off recovering at the ranch. We're set up to help wounded warriors both mentally and physically. In effect, she's a wounded warrior, having escaped her enemy. I'll speak with the doctor when he makes his rounds in the morning."

The nurse nodded. "Her bloodwork will be back when he makes his rounds, which will help him make any decisions regarding her treatment." She glanced at Jane. "We can't make her stay. And if being in the hospital is causing her more stress, a rehab ranch could be the answer." She gathered Jane's and Gus's dinner trays. "I take it you both will be staying through the night?"

Hannah and Gus nodded.

He wasn't going anywhere without Jane.

Nurse Foster left the room, returning shortly after with two blankets. She handed them to Gus and Hannah. "You might as well get some sleep. I'll be around if you need anything."

"Thank you," Hannah said.

Gus nodded to the lounger. "You can have the chair."

Her brow puckered. "Are you sure?"

He snorted. "Yeah."

After Hannah settled in the chair, she glanced up at Gus. "Aren't you going to settle?"

He shook his head. "Not yet." With too much adrenaline coursing through his veins, he needed to move. He paced the short length of the room and back.

"How long was she awake?" Hannah asked.

"At least forty-five minutes," he answered.

"Did she tell you her name?"

Gus shot a glance toward the closed door. "No. I told the nurse that her name was Jane Black and that I was her bodyguard. Otherwise, she wouldn't let me into the room. And as you can see, she needs someone in the room with her at all times. She insists she needs to get out of here." He shook his head. "Stubborn."

"Scared," Hannah said softly.

Gus's gut knotted. He hated that he couldn't wipe away her fear. If anything, he added to it when he got too close. "She told me how she got into the barn."

Hannah's eyebrows rose. "Oh, yeah?"

His lips turned up on the corners. "She stole into the horse trailer you brought Lady home in."

Hannah frowned. "How did we not see her?"

He shrugged. "She said the horse called to her. I didn't get much more from her. Could she have stowed away when you loaded the horse onto the trailer?"

Hannah shook her head. "We were out in an open field. We would've seen someone approaching us."

"Did you stop along the way back to the ranch?" he asked.

Her eyes narrowed. "We stopped at a truck stop in Livingston around eleven-thirty last night. We climbed into the trailer to check on Lady right before we left. There wasn't anyone in there with the mare."

"Could she have slipped in after you got out?"

"It's possible."

Gus strode for the door.

"Where are you going?"

"To call Hank Patterson. Most of those truck stops have surveillance cameras. If we can find her slipping into your horse trailer, we might be able to backtrack and see how she got to the truck stop."

He stepped into the hallway and called his boss, Stone Jacobs, down in West Yellowstone.

"Hey, Gus, how's the assignment? Has she regained consciousness?"

Gus ran a hand through his hair, wishing he had more information than he did. "She has."

"Who is she?"

"Don't know. She's not giving that information because she's afraid her captors will find her. She did say that she stowed away in the horse trailer Hannah and Taz used to bring home a rescue mare. They stopped at the truck stop in Livingston around eleven-thirty last night. Is it possible to get someone to go through their surveillance videos?"

"If they run it through their internet, anything's possible. Hold on." Stone's voice sounded as if in the distance, but Gus could make out what he was saying. "Kyla, can you dial Hank and Swede into this call?"

A female's voice responded.

Gus couldn't make out her words.

A moment later, another male voice said, "Hank, here."

"And Swede," said another.

"Whatcha got?" Hank asked.

Gus explained what little he'd learned from their client.

"On it," Swede said. Seconds later, he announced, "That franchise has their systems linked online from what I can see. I should be able to get in. It'll take some time, but between me and Kyla, we should be able to go through the images from last night fairly quickly."

"Still no name for our client?" Hank asked.

"No. She's afraid to give her name to anyone in case whoever held her captive finds her. She wants out of the hospital really bad. Hannah thinks we can move her to the rehab ranch if her blood tests come back good and the doctor releases her. She might be more willing to talk when she gets there."

"Your description of her that you gave us earlier isn't much to go on," Kyla's voice broke into the conversation. "Black hair, brown eyes and Native American brings up a disturbing number of missing girls and women from reservations in Montana, Idaho and Wyoming. All unsolved."

"If we could get a photo of her, we could run it

against those missing persons' reports," Swede said. "We're shooting in the dark."

"I'll work on it. The first thing that needs to happen is to get her out of the hospital and move her to the rehab ranch."

"You could bring her to White Oak Ranch," Hank offered. "Sadie would love the company."

"Thanks, Hank," Gus said. "But I think the rehab ranch might be better equipped to care for her. She's suffering from malnutrition and probably PTSD. Hannah and her crew are best suited to help her."

"True," Hank said. "Hannah works miracles with the two-legged and four-legged residents. If you need backup, we can be there in less than half an hour."

"Thanks," Gus said.

"We'll let you know if we find anything from the surveillance videos," Swede promised.

"And I'll let you know what we learn from her as soon as she opens up," Gus said. "Out here."

He ended the call and ducked back into the room.

Stretched out in the reclining chair with the hospital blanket pulled up to her chin, Hannah's gaze met his. "Anything?"

"They'll be reviewing the surveillance videos through the night."

She nodded. "We might as well get some sleep. Tomorrow could prove to be challenging."

Gus took the blanket and settled on the window seat cushions, leaning his back against the wall, his legs stretched out in front of him. "You think she'll refuse to go with us to the ranch?"

"I have no idea what she'll do." Hannah's gaze went to the woman sleeping on the bed beside her. "As scared as she is, she might want to disappear."

"You saw her," Gus said. "She couldn't walk out of here if she tried."

"After a good night's sleep and the nutrients they're feeding her through the IV, there's no telling what she'll be capable of." Hannah yawned.

"Where's Taz?" Gus asked.

She gave him a fleeting smile. "Camped out in the SUV in the hospital parking lot. He's keeping watch on the hospital entrance. If we need him, all we have to do is call."

Gus leaned his head against the wall, determined to sleep with one eye open, if at all. As a Navy SEAL, he'd learned how to rest and remain alert at the same time. His life and the lives of his teammates had depended on his ability to be ready for anything at any time.

He must have drifted off. A slight noise had him fully awake and on his feet in seconds.

The door to the hospital room swung open. A man dressed in hospital scrubs entered, carrying a container full of tubes, syringes and alcohol prep pads. He headed for the bed where Jane lay sleeping.

Gus stepped between him and the bed. "How do I know you work here?"

The man held up his hospital badge. "I'm just here to draw blood. The doctor will want the results when he does his rounds in a few hours."

Gus didn't move.

The man sighed. "Look, buzz the nurses. They can vouch for me. But make it quick. I have a dozen more to collect in the next hour."

Gus punched the call button. Moments later, Nurse Foster entered the room. Her gaze went from Gus to the lab tech. "It's okay," she spoke softly. "He's legit. Is that all you needed?"

"Yes, ma'am," Gus said.

The nurse left the room.

Gus stepped aside, allowing the man access to Jane, standing beside him as he worked.

The tech was quick. He applied the rubber tourniquet, located the vein and drew blood in under two minutes. Once he was done, he removed the rubber strap around Jane's arm, affixed labels to the tubes and slid them into slots in the basket he carried. "All done," he said. "Results will be available when the doctor comes through."

After the man left, Gus stood for a moment, staring down at the woman lying so still on the bed. Her dark hair and skin made a striking contrast against the white pillow and sheets. He'd bet it was beautiful when it was clean and combed.

Her eyes twitched behind her eyelids, and her

breathing became more erratic. She was headed into a nightmare.

Gus knew the feeling of dread, the horror of knowing something bad was about to happen and feeling helpless to stop it. He'd come to Brighter Days at Stone's suggestion when lack of sleep for over a week had left him walking around like a zombie.

Through sessions with Hannah and the hard work involved with ranching, he'd worked through the issues he'd buried inside. As he'd learned to accept what he couldn't change and to embrace a different life than what he'd trained so hard for, he'd been better able to cope with anxiety and the nightmares had faded.

How long would it take for Jane to overcome the horror she'd endured? Not a week, or a month. Maybe not even a lifetime.

Gus had no doubt that Hannah could help her if Jane would let her. She could never undo the past, but Hannah would help her realize that she was still young and had a life worth living.

He touched a finger to the back of her hand, wanting to tell her she'd be all right. Wishing she would believe him.

Why should she believe a man she'd just met?

Gus had never been raped. He didn't know how it felt to be so violently abused.

Her legs moved beneath the sheets, and her head

moved side to side. Her hand turned over, and her fingers curled around his.

He squeezed gently and leaned close. "Shhh," he breathed into her ear. "You're okay. I've got you. I won't let anyone hurt you."

She stilled.

Gus expected her eyes to open.

They didn't.

He continued speaking softly. "You're okay. I won't let anyone hurt you."

Her chest rose on a deep breath and sank as she let it out with a sigh. Her face and body relaxed. Soon, her breathing returned to a slow, steady pace.

She slept with her fingers still curled around his.

When Gus tried to pull free, her grip tightened.

If holding his hand made her feel safe enough to sleep, he'd stand by her bed the rest of the night.

"Hey," Hannah said behind him. "Take the lounger." She rose and motioned for him to sit. Then she laid the blanket over his lap.

"What about you?" he whispered.

"I can sleep anywhere," she said. "She needs you exactly where you are." Hannah laid on the window seat and pulled the other blanket up over her shoulders. Moments later, she was asleep.

Gus closed his eyes.

What felt like seconds later, the door to Jane's hospital room opened.

Nurse Foster entered. "Sorry to wake you, but we

need to turn on the light. The doctor is making his rounds, and he'll want to speak to Ms. Black."

The harsh lights blinked on.

Gus pushed to his feet but didn't leave the bedside.

Jane still held onto his hand.

Her eyelashes fluttered against her cheeks.

"Ms. Black," Nurse Foster called out, "how are you feeling this morning?"

"Like I could sleep another day," she said, her voice barely more than a croak.

"Dr. Rhodes is making his rounds early this morning. Technically, I'm off shift, but I stayed to catch him up on your case."

"Thank you," Jane whispered. "Did you tell him I need to leave?"

"I did. He wants to talk to you, so I thought I'd give you a heads-up." Nurse Foster smiled. "Can I raise your head?"

Jane nodded.

The nurse pressed the button, and the head of the bed rose.

As she moved to a sitting position, Jane looked around, her gaze coming to rest on Gus.

"Were you here all night?" she asked.

He nodded.

Her gaze dropped to her hand, where her fingers were entwined with his. Her brow dipped. When she pulled away, he didn't offer any resistance.

ELLE JAMES

Nurse Foster disappeared into the bathroom and emerged with a cloth and a basin of water. "Until the doctor says you can get up, you'll have to make do with a sponge bath." She set the basin on the rolling table, pulled a new brush from her pocket and handed it to Hannah. "Think you can manage the tangles?"

Hannah nodded, smothering a yawn. "Yes, ma'am."

The nurse turned to Gus and cocked an eyebrow. "Could Ms. Black have some privacy?"

"Yes, of course." He locked gazes with Jane.

Her eyes widened.

He held her gaze. "You're okay. I'll be right outside the door. I won't let anyone hurt you." He winked and tipped his head toward Hannah. "Except maybe Hannah. Those tangles will be a challenge."

Jane's hand rose to her matted hair, and her cheeks reddened.

"I'll be careful," Hannah said. "This will be new for me. I've worked with men for so long, and I never had a kid sister to practice on." She smiled at Jane. "I'll pretend you're my little sister." The therapist kept talking as she started to brush Jane's hair.

Gus backed through the door and let it swing shut. He planted himself in front of her door to keep anyone else from entering until a man in a white coat emerged from the room next to Jane's and headed his way.

"Is this Ms. Black's room?" he asked.

Gus nodded. "Yes, sir."

"You must be her bodyguard." He held out one hand and raised his hospital ID with the other. "I'm Dr. Rhodes."

Gus studied the ID, comparing the photo on the card with the man in the coat. When he was satisfied the man was who he said he was, he shook the doctor's hand. "They were giving Ms. Black a sponge bath," he said, stepping to the side to allow the doctor through.

Dr. Rhodes knocked on the door.

"Come in," Nurse Foster called out.

The doctor pushed through the door.

Gus looked in and waited.

"Mr. Walsh, Ms. Black says you can come in as well," the nurse called out.

He walked in and stood back while the doctor performed his examination, poking, prodding and listening to her chest. Then he stood back and asked Jane, "How are you feeling?"

"Better," she said.

With her face clean and the tangles smoothed from her hair, she looked like a different person. She even had some color in her cheeks. The dark circles beneath her eyes would take time to fade.

"Are you in any pain?" Dr. Rhodes asked.

She shook her head. "Only where I'm bruised."

He nodded. "I'm told you want to leave the hospital this morning."

Jane nodded.

"We gave you antibiotics in your IV, but I'm going to prescribe a full round of antibiotics to take for the next ten days. With what you've been through, it's a good idea, even though your labs came back clean."

Jane glanced at the nurse, her brow twisting.

Nurse Foster laid a hand on her shoulder. "Clean is good." She leaned closer and whispered. "No sexually transmitted diseases."

Though she whispered, Gus could make out her words.

Jane shot a glance toward him, her cheeks flaming, tears welling in her eyes.

Gus stood as if he were standing in formation at an inspection, eyes staring straight ahead, unmoving as if he hadn't heard the nurse's comment.

The doctor touched her hand and lowered his voice. "And you're not pregnant."

The tears building in Jane's eyes slipped over the edge and spilled down her cheeks.

Though he continued to stare straight ahead, Gus could see her reaction to the doctor's words. He fought to appear unaffected, when in truth, Jane's tears wrecked him.

He wanted to find the bastards who'd hurt her and punch them until their faces resembled hamburger meat. Then he wanted to string them up by their limp dicks and watch them scream in the same kind of pain they'd subjected her to.

"I know you're scared, and you have every right to be," the doctor said. "You need to see a mental health professional to help you reclaim your life. Just remember this...you are not to blame for what happened to you. You are not the one who should feel any shame. Live your life. Find happiness. If you do that, you don't let them win."

Jane scrubbed at the tears on her cheeks and nodded solemnly.

"Good." Dr. Rhodes stood back. "Now, I'll sign your discharge papers if you can walk to the door by yourself."

She glanced at the door, her eyes rounding worriedly. Her gaze darted from Hannah to the nurse and finally to Gus.

He nodded, wanting to tell her she could do it, but didn't. She had to know she would do it. On her own.

Jane squared her shoulders, tossed back the sheet and swung her legs over the side of the bed.

"It's not a race," the doctor said. "It's not how slow or fast you go that matters. You only have to make it to the door."

She nodded and slid off the bed onto her feet.

Still holding onto the bedrail, she stood still until her legs stopped shaking. Then she took one step, still holding on. Then another. At this point, she had to let go of the rail.

When she did, she swayed.

Gus tensed, ready to lunge forward and catch her if she fell.

She regained her balance and took another step, then another, and another until she reached the door.

"Congratulations," Dr. Rhodes said with a smile. "You just earned your discharge papers." He turned to the computer and keyed in his notes, giving Nurse Foster instructions as he did.

Jane sighed and leaned against the doorframe.

Gus moved forward and offered his elbow. He didn't reach for her or try to grab her. He gave her the choice of accepting his help or not.

Her knees wobbled slightly.

For a moment, he thought she'd try to make it back to the bed on her own and possibly fall in the process.

Gus was pleasantly surprised when she slipped her hand through the crook of his elbow and leaned against him.

He helped her back to the bed and up onto the mattress. "Good job," he whispered.

She dipped her head. "I had to. I can't stay here."

The doctor finished making his notes and turned to Jane. "Ms. Black, it's your choice what you want done with the evidence collected in your initial examination. You don't have to make that decision now. Take your time. When you're ready, let us know."

She nodded. "Thank you, Dr. Rhodes."

His mouth pressed into a tight line. "I'm sorry this happened to you." He shifted his gaze to Gus. "Keep her safe."

Gus nodded. "Yes, sir."

When the doctor left the room, Jane scooted to the edge of the bed. "Let's get out of here."

"Ms. Black." Nurse Foster gave her a stern look. "You might have walked to the door for the doctor, but the only way you're leaving this hospital is in a wheelchair."

"Oh, yeah?" Jane lifted her chin. "Just watch me." She pushed off the bed and landed on her feet. Her face paled, and she pitched forward.

Gus was there, catching her in his arms before she hit the floor. He held her against his chest until they both had their balance.

Jane rested her hands against his chest, her brow descending in a stubborn frown. "I'm fine," she said. "I don't need help."

Gus stared at her through narrowed eyes. "I suspect your stubborn streak is going to make my job to protect you a challenge."

"You have no idea," she said. "For that matter, you don't have to protect me. I can take care of myself. Besides, you'll only slow me down."

"From what?" he demanded.

Her mouth clamped shut.

"Still not talking?" He shook his head. "I can't

keep you safe if I don't know who and what I'm up against."

Her jaw tightened. She glanced past him as the door opened. "My ride is here."

Gus counted to ten in his head and turned to find an orderly with a wheelchair.

"She can't leave in a hospital gown," the nurse said. "Hang on. I might have something she can wear." Nurse Foster darted out of the room and returned carrying a set of blue hospital scrubs. "Everyone out while we get our girl changed out of that hospital gown."

Gus waited with the orderly in the hallway while the nurse and Hannah got Jane ready to leave the hospital.

Jane was weak and barely able to cross a room. Gus cringed at the thought of when she regained her strength. She'd be hard to keep up with.

They'd cross that bridge when they came to it. He hoped he had a little more time to chink away at her armor and get her to break her silence before she was at or near one hundred percent.

CHAPTER 7

PEYTON CHOMPED AT THE BIT, wanting to run out of the hospital, not be wheeled out in a chair like an invalid.

Unfortunately, she needed the chair. How she'd managed to run from the trailer was still very much a miracle. Her body had held up when she'd needed it most. Now, it was as if it had gone into hibernation mode, shutting down all systems to give herself time to regain her strength and expel the last effects of the drugs they'd given her.

With her body on hold, she was never more aware of the ticking clock counting down to the day Snake and his guys decided to clean house and do away with the women they still held captive.

She didn't have time to be weak. Those women needed her to be strong, to find and free them.

Peyton clenched her fists and banged them against her wobbly legs.

She shot a glance at Gus. She wanted to trust him. When they made it back to the rehab ranch, could she get up the courage to tell them who she was and why she was so determined to get out of the hospital and back to the trailers she'd escaped?

No.

Even if she trusted Gus, there were others at the ranch. Too many others. The more people she was around, the more chance of someone letting it slip where she was. She would be safer...the other women would be safer if Peyton Running Bear stayed lost. They wouldn't be looking for Jane Black. Hopefully, that would buy her time to regain her strength.

Once she could get around on her own without falling or passing out, she'd find the women and free them.

Her eyes narrowed. Maybe she'd get a gun.

Peyton had fired guns some of her guy friends had owned. That had been in a field, shooting at drink cans, not people.

If she came face-to-face with Snake, did she have the fortitude to pull the trigger?

Her teeth clenched.

Hell, yes! She'd shoot him in the knee first. Then, the other knee. Then, the groin. Rather than kill him outright, she'd stop there and watch as he bled out slowly, writhing in pain.

"Jane?" Gus's voice sounded close to her.

She pulled herself out of her morbid musings and looked up into Gus's face.

His was frowning. "Are you all right?"

She shook the last images of Snake dying in pain out of her mind and gave her bodyguard a tight smile. "I'm fine."

His brow wrinkled. "Really? What were you thinking about?"

She shrugged. "Stuff. Why?"

"You had the look of a psychopathic child about to rip the head off her sister's favorite doll."

She sighed. "You're not too far off. Actually, I was imagining the most painful way for someone to die."

"Not me, I hope," Gus said.

Peyton shook her head. "No. Not you."

"Sounds like we need to schedule some anger therapy sessions," Hannah said.

"I don't want to lose my anger," Peyton said. "Not yet."

"I didn't say you should." Hannah touched her shoulder. "Just that you might want help managing it so it doesn't take over."

Peyton *wanted* anger to take over. She'd need pure rage to fuel her fight.

They emerged from the hospital into a bright, sunny day.

As the wheelchair rolled to a stop outside the hospital door at the pickup point, Peyton raised her face to the sky, her heart swelling with the joy of feeling the sunshine on her cheeks and the tender touch of the breeze caressing her face.

Ready tears welled in her eyes. Some tipped over the edge and rolled down her cheeks.

"What's wrong?" Gus dropped to a squat beside her chair.

"Nothing." She swiped at the moisture on her cheeks.

"If it was nothing, then why the tears?" he asked softly.

She laughed, the sound catching on the sob rising in her throat. "I didn't think I'd ever see the sunshine again or feel the wind on my skin. I spent my childhood outdoors, running, playing in the sunshine and riding horses across the prairie. I didn't appreciate it nearly enough while I had it. Then one day, I didn't have the clean air, the sunshine or the freedom to ride across the prairie without a care in the world."

"I can't say that you'll get that back," Hannah warned. "But your experiences shape who you are. You change and hopefully grow wiser, stronger and even more capable of anything you set your mind to."

A large SUV rolled up in front of her and stopped.

A man jumped down from the driver's seat and rounded to the passenger side. "Are we ready to go?"

"Jane," Hannah said, "this is Taz, my husband."

'Hi, Jane." Taz smiled down at her. "We've met,

only you were out at the time. Glad to see you upright."

Hannah nodded toward the SUV. "I call shotgun."

"That leaves Gus and our guest in the back." Taz turned to Peyton. "Need help getting in?"

"No, thank you." Peyton couldn't rely on others to help her do all she needed to get done. She needed to build her strength. With the urgency of her recovery bearing down on her, she braced her hands on the armrests of the wheelchair and pushed to her feet.

Gus sprang to her side, bless his male testosterone.

Peyton abandoned her hold on the wheelchair armrests to wrap her hands around Gus's arm. "This is only temporary," Peyton whispered loud enough Gus could hear, but hopefully no one else. "It's the first step to regaining my life and independence."

"Until then, don't be shy," Gus said. "I'm no expert on physical or mental therapy, but Hannah is. And as a guest at the ranch, you have full access to her. She helped me when I was at my lowest. Let her help you."

Peyton's gaze went to the therapist as she leaned up on her toes and kissed Taz. Her heart contracted with envy. In the past, she'd always wanted what they seemed to have.

Love.

Now...

She'd never make love with a man again. How

could she when she'd been used and abused by so many? She was damaged goods.

Gus helped her up into the SUV. Once she was seated, he leaned across her and secured her seatbelt.

Peyton held her breath until Gus snapped the buckle in place and settled into his own seat beside her.

He'd been so close she could feel the heat of his body. That closeness had almost overwhelmed her. But his sexy scent held her in place long enough to fully appreciate his sandalwood and fresh air aromas.

Yes, he smelled amazing.

Not like the sleazy men who'd paid Snake for the privilege of fucking drugged women.

Once they were seated and buckled in, Taz pulled out of the parking lot and onto a highway. He headed out of Bozeman and into the morning sun toward the Brighter Days Rehab Ranch.

"Hannah," Peyton said softly.

"Yes," Hanna responded.

Peyton stared out at the landscape in front of the vehicle. "I need to be able to walk and run as soon as possible."

"I can help you," Hannah said. "Just don't expect miracles."

Peyton cocked an eyebrow. "Your friend here says you work miracles."

"Sweetie, even miracles take time," Hannah reminded her.

"Can we speed up the process?" Peyton asked.

Hannah chuckled. "I could, but will your muscles be ready?" She glanced over her shoulder at Peyton. "We'll do our best."

"Thank you," Peyton said, settling back in her seat, her shoulder touching Gus's, glad for the warmth. He made her feel safe in a world that had been brutal.

During the long drive, Taz and Hannah discussed the ranch, their voices lulling Peyton into a trance.

One moment, she was staring at the road ahead.

Surely, she'd only blinked...

The next moment, they were pulling up to a ranch house.

She'd fallen asleep, leaning against Gus's shoulder.

Gus got out of the SUV and held the door for her.

Peyton scooted to the edge of the seat and looked down at the ground that seemed so far away.

Gus held out his arms. "It's okay to lean on someone every once in a while. At least until you're feeling better. Stop fighting it."

She sighed and let him help her to the ground. Her feet had barely touched the cool, damp earth when Gus swept her up into his arms.

"We need to get you some clothes and shoes," he said.

"I have some things she can wear," Hannah said. "Shoes might be an issue if we're not the same size."

"Where are we going?" Gus asked.

"Up the stairs, turn right. Take her to the second

door on the left. It's the yellow room. You can have the blue room next to it."

Peyton draped her arm around his neck, too tired to argue and too weak to climb any stairs.

The man took her up the stairs without breaking a sweat or breathing hard. Once at the top, he followed Hannah's directions, pushing a door open into a room decorated with a yellow theme.

A white iron bed took up most of the room, with an antique dresser against one wall. A floral-patterned wing-back chair sat near a set of French doors. The pastel yellow comforter was sprinkled with a white daisy pattern that made Peyton smile. Everything about the room made her glad to be there and ready to burrow beneath the blanket and sleep until she woke from the nightmare that had claimed her life for so many months.

Gus laid her on the bed and stepped back.

Hannah entered the room carrying a stack of clothes. "These are a few things I grabbed. I'll look through the rest of my things later. The clothes might be too long since you're petite, but it's better than nothing. We'll have to get someone to pick up some shoes in Bozeman. Mine will be too big for your little feet." She cocked her head to one side. "Do you want something to eat, or would you rather go back to sleep?"

Peyton's head spun with the amount of energy

Hannah exhibited. "I don't mean to be anti-social, but I'd rather sleep."

Hannah helped her slide beneath the sheets and comforter, tucking it around her. "I'll bring you some water and a plate of crackers and cheese in case you wake up and want a little something to tide you over until lunch."

"Thank you," Peyton said. "I don't mean to be a burden on you. As soon as I'm able, I'll move on."

"To where?" Hannah asked, her brow wrinkling.

Peyton hadn't thought that far ahead. Where could she go? Until Snake and his buddies were caught and jailed, she wasn't safe back on the rez. Even if it was safe, her aunt and uncle hadn't wanted her when she'd come to live with them after her parent's deaths. Peyton pinched the bridge of her nose, her head aching at the thought that she was as good as homeless.

Hannah touched her arm. "Don't worry about it now. You're welcome to stay here as long as you like. We're a refuge. We take in animals and people who need a second chance in the world." She smoothed a strand of Peyton's hair back from her forehead.

"Sleep will help to reset your body."

Peyton closed her eyes, her last sight that of Gus silhouetted against the light coming through the windows of the French doors.

His presence made her heart beat faster.

Out of fear?

No.

It was something else. Her mind was still too fuzzy for her to put a finger on it. All she knew was it wasn't the gut-twisting fear she felt at the possibility of being caught by Snake.

Deep inside, she believed that she didn't have to be afraid of Snake with the big Navy SEAL standing guard.

Peyton rolled onto her side and curled into a ball. A thought flitted through her consciousness as she slipped into a deep sleep. With Gus around, she wasn't afraid for her life...but her heart might be in danger.

CHAPTER 8

GUS STOOD FOR A LONG TIME, watching Jane as she lay nestled in the yellow comforter on the white iron bed. The room was light, feminine and, in a strange way, soothing to the soul. He was glad Hannah had assigned this room to Jane. Hopefully, the colors and sentiment would help draw Jane out enough to tell them more about her and where she was from.

The truck stop where she'd stowed away in the horse trailer was on the border of Montana and Wyoming, due north of Yellowstone National Park. If she was from any reservation in Wyoming, it was probably Wind River.

While Jane slept, Gus texted Swede.

Gus: Anything on the video surveillance footage?

Swede: Still reviewing. Found the horse trailer. It's tucked between eighteen-wheelers. No clear view of the side door. Expanding search around the area.

Multiple cameras. Will focus missing persons search on Wind River. Still need photo of Jane.

Feeling like a sleazy peeping Tom, Gus snapped a photo of Jane lying against a pillow in peaceful repose. He quickly sent it to Swede, pocketed his cell phone and dropped into the chair.

With less than three hours of sleep the night before, Gus closed his eyes to rest them.

A soft knock against wood jerked him awake, sending him to his feet in seconds.

The bedroom door eased open.

Hannah stepped inside, carrying a tray. "As much as she needs sleep, she needs to eat to fuel her body." She spoke in a whisper. "I hate to wake her."

"It's okay," Jane said. "I'm awake." She opened her eyes, staring up at the ceiling for a moment before turning her head toward Hannah. "You don't have to wait on me," Jane said. "I don't want to be a burden."

Hannah smiled. "It's no trouble. I thought you might like to have lunch up here. The guys can get rowdy at the table."

Jane nodded. "Thanks."

Gus took the tray from Hannah and laid it on the small table beside the chair while Hannah adjusted the pillows behind Jane's head, helping her to sit up. "After lunch, I can help you if you want to get a bath."

Jane's eyes widened. "I'd love that. But I can—"

"Don't even think about going solo," Hannah cut her off. "I don't mind helping. And I'd feel better knowing you haven't fallen and cracked open your skull or slipped beneath the surface and drowned."

Jane's lips twitched. "I get the picture. No dying on the premises. Thank you."

Hannah nodded to Gus.

He carried the tray over to Jane and settled it on her lap.

"Lunch isn't anything fancy, just a grilled cheese sandwich and tomato soup." Hannah lifted a cloth napkin beside the plate and draped it over Jane's chest. "For me, it's comfort food."

Jane's brow wrinkled as she stared at the food on the tray. "My mom used to make grilled cheese and tomato soup when I was little. Mostly because we couldn't afford much else, but it was warm and filling. I never thought we were poor," she said, her voice softening, "as long as we had each other."

Jane's head drooped. She stared at the food without touching it, possibly not even seeing it.

Gus would guess Jane's mother was no longer with her.

"Did your siblings like grilled cheese and tomato soup as well?" Gus asked, fishing for more information about this beautiful waif of a woman who'd suffered so much.

"No siblings," she said. "Just me and Mom. Until it was just me."

"I'm sorry," Hannah said. "So often, our mothers are more than the women who brought us into the world. They're our best friends, confidants and protectors. I miss my mother every day. She's been gone for five years now, but not a day goes by that I don't reach for the phone to call her with a question or to share something cool. How long has your mother been gone?"

"Fifteen years," Jane whispered.

Hannah's brow knitted. "You couldn't have been more than thirteen or fourteen years old."

"Twelve," Jane said and looked away.

The devastation still echoed in the shadows of her eyes.

Gus wanted to pull her into his arms and make everything all right, even though he knew he couldn't. First, pulling her into his arms might frighten her. Second, Jane's mother wouldn't come back from the dead. For that matter, no one could undo the things that had happened to her during her captivity.

Just like no amount of second-guessing could undo the fact that his friend had died in his arms in Afghanistan.

His past had been written in stone. His present and future were blank slates. What could happen was up to him. Yes, he should remember the past, but not let it be his sole focus like it had been for too long.

Jane couldn't change her past. She couldn't unlive the abuse she'd endured. But she had a future to live.

It was up to Gus to make sure her past didn't

repeat itself, that the people who'd held her captive didn't do it again.

If he had his way...if he got the chance...he'd make sure they never abused another woman. Scum like that didn't deserve to live. They weren't redeemable in any way.

"I need to check on our newest resident in the barn," Hannah said. "I'll be back in thirty minutes to help you with that bath. That should give you time to finish your lunch."

After Hannah left the room, an awkward silence settled between Gus and Jane.

Jane dipped the spoon into the tomato soup. "Have you had lunch?"

Gus shook his head. "I can eat later."

"You don't have to stay while I eat." Jane's cheeks flushed a light pink. "I'm sure you have better things to do than babysit me. Besides, I think I'll be safe on my own for a few minutes."

He gave her a crooked smile in an attempt to set her more at ease. "Are you trying to get rid of me already?" With a sigh, he pressed a hand to his chest. "You wound me. And here I thought I was being gentlemanly and protective."

Her eyes widened. "Oh, you have been all that. I just don't like being a bother."

He leaned forward, resting his elbows on his knees. "Jane, you're not a bother." He frowned. "If I've said or done anything that makes you think you're bothering me, I apologize. I only want to help. If anything, I'm probably bothering you by hovering."

Her chin dipped, and her lips quirked on the corners. "You are hovering a bit. And it's hard to eat when you're the only one in the room with food." She looked up. "I can't possibly eat the entire cheese sandwich. Rather than sit there watching me eat, why don't you take half and join me?" She cut the sandwich in half and handed one side to him with a challenging lift of one eyebrow.

His stomach rumbled. "You should eat that."

"It's too much. I'd hate for it to be wasted." She continued to hold it out. "Please, don't make me eat alone."

Gus took the proffered offering. "Thanks." If eating half her sandwich made her more comfortable, he'd do it. He bit into the bread and melted cheese and sighed.

"It's good, isn't it?" she said after she chewed and swallowed her first bite.

He nodded. "Like you said, it reminds me of home. Is it a law that mothers feed their children grilled cheese sandwiches, or do they do it as a rite of passage?"

"I think both," Jane said.

"Whatever, it's like tasting home." He took another bite.

"Where's home for you?" Jane asked.

"It used to be on a farm in Indiana," he said.

Her brow furrowed. "I'm sorry."

He laughed. "Why? It was a lot of work for little profit."

"No, that's not what I meant." A flush of pink rose up her neck. "I'm sorry for your loss."

His brow puckered. "My loss?" Then he realized what she was saying and shook his head. "No loss at all. My parents are alive and kicking. They sold the farm a few years ago and moved to Florida. My dad never wanted to shovel snow again or fix a broken tractor. They live in a senior community where the hardest work he has to do is mow a little patch of grass once a week."

Jane smiled. "Sounds like heaven. How often do you see them?"

"At least once a year, sometimes more."

She laid her sandwich on the plate and lifted the spoon again. "Any siblings?"

He nodded, hoping that sharing his life with her would help her to open up about hers. "Two brothers."

"Are they in Florida as well?"

He shook his head. "John joined the Army right out of high school. He's still on active duty, stationed in Germany. Ross went to the Air Force Academy. He's a pilot in the Air Force, stationed in Texas."

"And you joined the Navy?"

Gus nodded.

One of her eyebrows lifted. "A boy from a land-locked state?"

He shrugged. "I wanted to be closer to water to see what all the fuss was about."

Her brow remained cocked, and she didn't say anything. It was as if she could see through his flippant response.

"Okay, it wasn't just the water that drew me. I'd heard about the Navy SEALs, the training they had to endure and the missions they performed. I wanted to be one of them. I wanted to make a difference."

"And did you?" she asked softly, "Did you make a difference?"

He looked away. "We took out some terrorists who'd done horrible things, so I guess we did make a little bit of a difference."

"But?" she prompted.

Gus stared at the door, seeing the past, not the wood paneling. "It was always at a cost."

Silence stretched between them.

When he looked back at Jane, she was staring at the bowl of soup, the spoon hovering but not moving.

He wasn't helping to lift her spirits by bringing her down with his depressing stories. "I contend that eating tomato soup with a spoon is ridiculous."

She glanced up, her brow furrowed. "How else do you eat it?"

"It's liquid; therefore, you don't eat it...you drink

it." He lifted his chin. "Ditch the spoon and drink it straight from the bowl."

Her lips twisted. "I thought that was something only children did when Mom wasn't looking."

"I won't tell if you won't." He winked.

Jane laid down her spoon, lifted the bowl and drank. When she laid the bowl down again, she had a bright red mustache of soup across her bottom lip.

Gus chuckled, reached over and grabbed the napkin from across her chest, his knuckles brushing against a breast.

She stiffened.

He almost froze but decided to pretend he hadn't touched her there and continued with the napkin to wipe her upper lip. "There. Now, no one will know you drank instead of using the spoon. And look how much you consumed. You'd still be spooning for the next hour to consume that much."

Jane laughed. "I haven't drunk from a soup bowl since I was maybe five years old."

"Sweetheart, you've been missing out." He held up his hands. "Just saying. Life's short. Drink from the soup bowl."

Jane was still smiling when Hannah returned for her tray.

"Wow," Hannah said. "Your appetite must be improving."

Gus winked at Jane behind Hannah's back.

Jane smothered a giggle.

The sound warmed Gus's heart. Her dark hair and Native American features made her strikingly beautiful. And her smile transformed her features, making them glow.

His heart skipped several beats and then thundered hard to catch up. He wasn't sure what was happening, but the intensity of that feeling scared him.

Gus pushed to his feet. "You'll be wanting that bath now. I'll leave you to it. If you need me, just yell. I'll be around." Then, like a cat with his tail on fire, he bolted from the room.

Once away from Jane's deep brown eyes and radiant smile, Gus slowed, and his pulse returned to normal.

Had he just had an anxiety attack? He shook his head. If it was, it wasn't like any of the others he'd experienced. Most of his attacks came on without warning or triggers,

This time, a woman's smile seemed to have set him off, making his heart race.

No. No. No.

It had to be a coincidence that the attack had followed Jane's radiant smile. There was no other reason that made any sense.

The only problem with the theory was that Gus didn't believe in coincidence.

CHAPTER 9

WHEN PEYTON WOKE the next morning, she wasn't sure she was awake. The room where she lay was something out of a fantasy where she was the princess waking in a castle, safe from her evil enemies.

She stretched, her skin sliding across crisp, clean sheets that smelled of fabric softener and fields of flowers. Beneath her, the mattress was soft. The yellow comforter with white daisies cheered her simply by looking at it.

Yes, she was still dreaming.

If she closed her eyes and opened them again, would all this beauty disappear? Would she be back in that nasty trailer, lying on a soiled mattress, wishing she was dead?

Peyton didn't want to close her eyes, but she had to know. With one long, last look, she stared around the room, drinking in the beauty, comfort and peace it represented, and then lowered her eyelids.

Her breath caught and held as she counted to three.

One.

Two.

Three.

As she opened her eyes for the second time, she let go of the breath in a sigh. It was real.

Her eyes filled. Tears slipped from the corners. She was blessed. Truly blessed and thankful for the people looking out for her.

She moved her arms and legs, testing her strength and coordination. The truer test would be when she stood. But she wasn't ready to try yet. At that moment, she felt so much better than she had in a long time. The brain fog had dissipated. She could think more clearly than she had since she'd been abducted on the side of the road all those months ago.

Sun streamed through the window, a silent reminder that it was the second day since she'd escaped the trailers. Two days had passed, and she was no closer to helping the others she'd left behind.

With a sigh, she flung back the covers and swung her legs over the side of the bed.

After falling so many times the day before, she feared being overly optimistic.

The ticking clock in her head made her square her shoulders and push to her feet.

Fully expecting to fall on her face, she was pleasantly surprised when her legs didn't wobble, and she maintained her balance. Encouraged, she took a step forward.

So far, so good.

Another step yielded the same results. Several more, and she made it to the bathroom. Relief filled her chest. She wasn't strong enough to run a marathon, but she could get around unassisted. She was amazed at what food and rest had done to revive her—that and the time she'd needed for the effects of the drugs in her body to fade.

She entered the bathroom, closed the door behind her, relieved herself and washed her face. Hannah had provided a brand-new hairbrush, toothpaste and a toothbrush.

As she leaned against the sink, she brushed the tangles from her hair then brushed her teeth. During the bath Hannah had helped her with, she'd cleaned her hair and skin, but no amount of soap or shampoo, baths or showers, would ever make her feel clean inside. What those men had done to her left her feeling permanently dirty.

She might get on with her life, but she doubted she'd ever feel comfortable with a man's touch.

Her thoughts went to Gus. He'd caught her when

she'd fallen and had carried her when she couldn't walk.

She hadn't shrunk away from him. That gave her a slim margin of hope.

As if thinking of him conjured the man, his voice called out through the bathroom door, "Jane?" Footsteps sounded, and a knock tapped on the door. "Are you all right in there?"

"I am," she responded. She set the toothbrush on the counter, checked her reflection in the mirror and glanced down at the nightgown Hannah had given her to wear. Though the fabric was light and floaty, it covered all the right places, falling to mid-thigh.

Not that it mattered what she wore. Gus had seen her in less.

She opened the door with a smile. "Good morning."

He frowned down at her. "You should've waited until someone could help you."

"I did fine." She walked past him, turned and held out her arms. "See? I'm steadier on my feet today. I can get around on my own."

His brow remained creased. "Don't get ahead of yourself. You don't want to fall and break something. It takes longer to recover from a broken bone."

She nodded. "Noted. I'll be careful." The scent of bacon drifted through the open door of her bedroom. "Am I too late for breakfast?" She rested a hand on her belly. "I'm hungry."

Finally, the frown creasing his forehead cleared, and Gus relaxed. "Cookie saved a plate for you. It's warming in the oven. Do you need help getting dressed?"

Her brows rose. "Are you offering?"

He shook his head. "Of course not. Hannah said to let her know if you need assistance."

Peyton shook her head. "I can manage on my own."

When he didn't make a move to leave the room, she cocked an eyebrow.

He straightened. "Right. I'll be on the other side of the door. Yell if you need me."

"Thanks." She waited for him to close the door behind him, tempted to yell just to see if he came rushing in.

She resisted the urge, knowing he would come crashing through, expecting the worst.

With a smile, she searched the closet where Hannah had hung the clothes she'd loaned her.

Her hand skimmed past the dresses. She selected a pair of jeans and a blue chambray blouse, pulled them on and stood in front of the full-length mirror affixed to the back of the bedroom door.

She laughed at her reflection.

"What's so funny?" Gus asked, his voice muffled by the door.

"I look like a little kid playing dress-up in her mother's clothes."

She was painfully thin and a lot shorter than the woman the clothes belonged to. The shirt was too long, the tails reaching halfway down her thighs. Tucked into the jeans and with the sleeves rolled up made it better. The jeans required the belt Hannah had thoughtfully provided to keep them from sliding off Peyton's hips. She cinched the belt to the last notch, then sat in the chair and rolled the five extra inches of fabric on the legs up to her ankles.

She pulled on a pair of boot socks and shook her head at the boots Hannah had left inside the door. They were several sizes too big. If she attempted to walk in them, she'd end up tripping and falling.

She didn't have shoes or a bra, but the clothes covered her body and kept her warm. Peyton wrapped her arms around herself, grateful for Hannah's generosity and determined to repay her kindness.

Her hand hovered over the doorknob.

Gus waited on the other side. She wondered if she should have chosen a dress. As it was, she looked like a child in hand-me-down clothes.

It didn't matter. She wasn't there to make a fashion statement. What she looked like did not matter. Those other women did.

As soon she was strong enough...

What?

She'd go charging into the trailer camp, demanding they let the other women go?

Peyton closed her eyes.

She didn't know what she'd do. Just that she had to do something.

"Jane?"

Gus's warm tones melted through the door panel, bringing her back to the present.

She might not know what she was going to do, but she'd figure it out. She would not let the difficulty of what she had to do overwhelm her. She'd escaped for a reason.

When she gripped the doorknob, it twisted beneath her fingers.

"Jane?" Gus eased the door open. When he saw her standing there, his brow dipped. "Why didn't you answer?"

"I—" When Peyton saw Gus looking at her with concern in his eyes, she didn't feel so alone. "I'm ready..." Ready to face her fears? To storm into hell and bring those women out?

Peyton forced a smile. "I'm ready for breakfast."

He offered her his arm, the gesture so quaint, old-fashioned and exactly what she needed.

She slid her hand through the crook of his elbow.

He turned toward the staircase. "First, breakfast, then what?" His arm tightened, bringing her hand against his side. "Conquer the world?"

"Yeah," she said. "Something like that."

Gus helped her down the stairs, one riser at a time.

With each step, she realized her strength was returning, along with her resolve. At the bottom of the stairs, she nodded, a sense of accomplishment swelling inside.

"You're doing great," Gus assured her.

"Thanks. It feels good to get around on my own," she said.

He led her into the kitchen, where Cookie stood at a counter, kneading a huge lump of dough.

"Your breakfast is in the warmer," he said. "Help yourself."

Gus pulled a glass out of a cabinet and set it on the counter in front of Peyton. "I'll get the food out of the warmer. You decide what you want to drink. There are juices and milk in the refrigerator, and coffee is always available on the counter by the door."

All the options sounded great when all she'd been given to drink for months was bottled water.

Peyton finally settled on milk, pouring some into the glass Gus had provided.

He pulled the covered dish from the warming oven and carried it to the large table that could seat a dozen people.

Peyton followed with her glass of milk.

After he set her plate on the table, he held her chair and waited for her to take her seat.

"I'll get utensils and a cup of coffee," he said and turned away.

"I don't want coffee," Peyton said.

"For me," he clarified.

Her cheeks heated.

Gus returned a moment later with a fork, knife and a cup of steaming coffee. He took the seat across from her and sipped his coffee while she dug into fluffy yellow eggs, bacon and toast.

Hannah entered the kitchen, carrying a basket full of eggs. "Oh, good. You're awake."

Peyton swallowed the bit of eggs she'd been chewing. "Yes, thank you for the clothes."

Hannah frowned. "I figured my things would swamp you, but wow. Taz is on his way to Bozeman as we speak. He'll pick up some things that will fit you better." She held up a hand. "Don't worry, he won't be shopping. I have a friend there who owns a clothing store. I called her this morning and asked her to select some things for you. I guessed at your size and asked her to look in the petite section. What I couldn't guess at was what size shoe you wear."

"Six," Peyton said. "But I don't have any money to pay her."

"Don't worry. Hank Patterson told me to put it on his tab. In fact, his wife Sadie is sending over some of her clothes and shoes. She's closer to you in size than I am, and she has an amazing wardrobe from the movies she's been in."

"Movies?" Peyton asked.

"Hank's wife is Sadie McClain," Hannah said. "You know. Hollywood's sweetheart?"

Peyton's eyes widened. "The movie star, Sadie McClain?"

Hannah grinned. "That's the one. She and Hank grew up together. They were high school sweethearts. Whatever clothes she sends should be fun. Hopefully, there will be some shoes or boots that will fit. I'll give her a call and let her know your shoe size."

Hannah left the room to make that call.

"Now, I know I've landed in some alternate reality," Peyton whispered.

Gus chuckled. "I was just as surprised that Hank Patterson was married to Sadie McClain."

Peyton forgot about the food on her plate. "Have you met her?"

He nodded. "Hank and Sadie came down to West Yellowstone to meet with my boss, Stone Jacobs, after a big job we worked on the Wind River Reservation in Wyoming."

Peyton's eyes widened. "Wind River?"

"You know it?" Gus asked.

Her heart skipped several beats. Now would be the time she could confess to Gus who she really was and that she was from the Wind River Reservation.

She opened her mouth to do that when the back door to the kitchen opened, and two men entered, arguing about sports teams. The guy leading the way had shaggy blond hair and green eyes. When he spotted Peyton, he grinned. "Vasquez, look. It's the girl Gus caught in the barn."

A dark-haired young man stepped up beside the blond and studied Peyton, his eyes narrowed. "Are you sure?"

The blond nodded. "It's her, isn't it, Gus?"

Gus glared at the two men. "Jane, these two men who lack in manners make up for it with their work ethic." He nodded to the blond. "Brody Franklin and Xavier Vasquez, this is Jane."

Peyton nodded as her cheeks heated and her gut tightened. How much did these men know about her? Did they know why she'd been hiding in the barn or where she'd come from? Had Gus or Hannah told them? Would they judge her or worse...expect her to be the whore she'd been forced to be?

Brody stuck out his left hand. That's when Peyton realized he was missing his right arm. She shook his left hand awkwardly.

When Xavier held out his right hand, Peyton noted that this man was missing his left arm.

Neither man held onto her hand too long nor said anything that indicated they knew her dirty secret.

"We're glad to see you up and around." Brody grinned. "You had ol' Gus scared when you passed out on him."

Gus's eyes narrowed. "Don't you two have work to do somewhere?"

"We do. We just came in to ask Hannah which horse she wants us to work with next."

"Jazzy," Hannah said as she entered the kitchen. "She could use the exercise. Oh, and could you bring George and Gracie in from the pasture and get them ready for a ride? I'd like to get Jones and Smallwood to work with them." She faced Peyton. "Do you ride?"

Peyton's heart flipped. "I used to."

Hannah grinned. "Sweetie, once you learn, you don't forget. It's like riding a bicycle, right?"

"A bicycle with a personality," Brody murmured.

"And the personality depends on the horse," Xavier added.

Peyton's mouth twitched. "That about sums it up."

"Would you like to ride today?" Hannah's brow dipped. "That is if you're up to it."

Peyton grinned. "I'd love to."

"I don't know." Gus frowned heavily. "Is it a good idea for her to be up on a horse so soon?"

"She doesn't have to walk or run. The horse does all that work," Hannah said. "Besides, working with and riding horses is therapy. You, of all people, should know that."

"She has to stay on," Gus pointed out. "That takes effort."

"She could walk the horse around the barnyard," Hannah suggested.

Peyton watched the two negotiate what she could or couldn't do and finally interrupted. "I'm still here."

Gus and Hannah turned to her.

"Sorry," Hannah said. "You're right. We can't make that decision for you. You can decide for yourself if you feel physically able."

"I'm able," Peyton said.

Hannah clapped her hands. "Perfect. By the time the guys have the horses brushed and saddled, Sadie's care package should be here. She's sending over a pair of boots in a size six that she wore in her last movie, along with jeans and shirts that should be a closer fit."

Brody and Xavier left the kitchen with their marching orders, and Hannah went to check on one of the guests who had a question.

Cookie had separated the dough into smaller lumps and left it to rise. "I'm headed to the grocery store in Eagle Rock. Do you need anything?"

Peyton shook her head. "Not me."

"Nothing here," Gus said.

When Cookie left, Gus and Peyton were alone again.

"I don't want to tell you what you can or can't do," Gus said. "I'm just worried about you being on a horse so soon."

Peyton leaned across the table and touched his hand. "Thank you for worrying, Gus. It's like Hannah called it. I want to ride. I used to ride all the time. It was the only time I felt completely free."

He turned his hand over and curled his fingers around hers. "Okay. As long as you take it slowly."

She smiled. "I will."

"And you finish your breakfast. You need all the energy you can get."

Her smile twisted. "What? Are you my mother, bargaining with me to eat my broccoli?"

Gus nodded. "Whatever it takes."

"Done." She pulled her hand free of his, finished eating the eggs, toast and bacon on her plate and downed the glass of milk.

"I still think it's a bad idea," Gus grumbled.

"A deal's a deal," Peyton said.

"Yeah." Gus pushed to his feet, gathered Peyton's plate and utensils and headed for the sink.

Peyton collected her glass and his mug and followed. "I'll wash these."

"Better yet," Gus said. "I'll wash. You can dry." He handed her a dry dishtowel and slid the dishes into the warm, soapy water Cookie had left in the sink. Together, they washed and dried the last of the breakfast dishes and placed them in the correct cabinet.

Working beside Gus performing such domestic functions felt natural. He didn't tell her she had to do the work or criticize her if it wasn't exactly how he thought it should be done.

After her mother had passed from the overdose, her aunt and uncle on her father's side had taken her in. As her only living relatives, the tribal council had told them they had to take her in. They'd resented her from the first day and used her as their private maid. After all, she had to "earn her keep."

Doing dishes with Gus was a pleasant task, shared equally. By the time they hung the dishtowels, a truck arrived to deliver a box from the White Oak Ranch.

"That's Hank and Sadie's place," Gus said.

They stepped onto the front porch as the ranch hand pulled a box out of the back seat.

Gus hurried down the steps to take the box from the man.

"Ms. McClain said not to worry about returning the items," the young man said. "She said keep them if you like or give them away."

"Please thank Sadie for her kindness," Peyton said from the top of the steps.

"Will do, ma'am," the cowboy said with a tip of his hat. Then he climbed into the truck and drove away.

Gus carried the box into the house and up the stairs to the yellow bedroom with Peyton close on his heels, handling the stairs with only a little effort.

Once he'd deposited the box on the bed, Gus backed out of the room.

"I'll only be a few minutes," Peyton said, eager to dig into the box of clothes from a famous movie star.

When she got the other women free, she'd share the items gladly. In the meantime, she'd have clothes that fit. As she sifted through the box, she smiled. There were boots and a lacy bra.

Feeling like a kid at Christmas, Peyton smiled as she stripped out of Hannah's clothes and dressed in the jeans, bra and long-sleeved cable-knit sweater. Everything fit perfectly. In just a few minutes, she was dressed in Sadie McClain's clothes, standing in front of the mirror, feeling almost like a million dollars.

True, what you looked like on the outside didn't change who you were on the inside, but it made Peyton feel better.

And she was going to ride a horse for the first time since her friend had sold his pony so long ago. Hope bloomed inside Peyton. Things were looking up. She tamped down her rising optimism, knowing from experience that good times were always followed by bad.

And the bad was coming. She could feel it all the way to her soul.

She couldn't stop it from happening like she couldn't stop her mother from dying, but she could be more prepared, starting with asking Gus where she could get a gun.

CHAPTER 10

THE SECOND TIME Jane stepped out of her bedroom that morning, it was like seeing two different people.

Gus blinked.

She wore jeans that hugged the swell of her hips like they were made for her. The cream-colored sweater clung to her breasts and torso, accentuating every curve, and contrasted beautifully with her dark hair. The boots completed the outfit, making Peyton appear like a model for western-wear apparel.

She met his gaze with a smile. "Better?"

"I liked the first outfit," he murmured. He liked it because it had made her look like a child. Which, in turn, made her less tempting. He spun away and walked to the top of the stairs.

Peyton followed, her smile fading. "You don't have to be so grumpy. Ms. McClain was very generous to send clothes."

"My apologies," Gus said. "I'm just worried about you riding." Which wasn't a lie. It just wasn't the whole truth. He was worried about his growing attraction to a woman whose real name he still didn't know.

They descended the stairs together.

Peyton seemed to be well on her way to recovering. Much quicker than Gus had anticipated. Which made him worry even more. He'd promised to keep her safe, but she hadn't promised to let him. He had a feeling she'd bolt as soon as she could.

He couldn't blame her.

Jane's fear of being caught and forced back into the sex trade was a good reason for her to want to keep moving.

Gus had to convince her he could help her if she trusted him with the truth.

At the barn, Franklin and Vasquez had two horses ready for Jane and Gus, saddled, bridled and ready to mount.

"We pulled Miss Daisy for Jane and Moriarty for you, Gus," Franklin announced.

Jane approached the sorrel mare. "Hey, sweet girl. How are you today?"

Gus studied Moriarty with a jaundiced eye.

"Don't worry, we fed him sweet feed; he should be in a good mood," Franklin said.

Gus frowned. "He's been less than consistent lately."

Vasquez approached Moriarty and ran a hand along his neck. "I lunged him for fifteen minutes before brushing and saddling him. He should be good."

"And Miss Daisy is an angel as always," Franklin said. "I'd trust this horse with a baby."

"She is the gentlest horse on the ranch," Vasquez vouched. "Have you ever ridden a horse?" he asked of Jane.

Jane smiled as she ran her hand along Daisy's neck and scratched behind her ear. "I used to ride bareback across the prairie all summer."

"I can't vouch for Daisy riding bareback, but she's the horse I would put a kid on," Vasquez said.

"She's that gentle," Franklin added.

Gus knew Miss Daisy. Whenever Hannah introduced a resident with no riding experience to the horses, she assigned Miss Daisy to that resident. Miss Daisy was gentle and patient. She'd never thrown a guest or acted up.

Now, Moriarty was another story altogether. Fortunately, Gus was a skilled horseman. His upbringing on a farm in Indiana had included years of riding, along with driving tractors from the ripe old age of seven.

"Is this your idea of one last jab at the old guy?" Gus asked Franklin.

"Not at all." Franklin gave him that innocent look

that might have swayed his grandmother but didn't convince Gus for a second.

Still, Gus could handle Moriarty, and Daisy was a perfect match for Jane. They could make a few circles around the barnyard and maybe a couple of passes in the small pasture. Daisy would be the perfect mount for Jane, and Gus would keep Moriarty in check should he get a wild hair up his ass.

Gus joined Jane next to Daisy. "Are you sure you've regained enough of your strength to ride?"

In answer, Jane planted her booted foot in Daisy's stirrup and swung up into the saddle. She smiled down at Gus. "Yes."

Gus had to admit Jane appeared comfortable and confident in the saddle.

He eyed Moriarty. "Don't pull any of your shenanigans today, man," he whispered into the gelding's ear. "We have to look out for Jane and Daisy."

The gelding tossed his head and danced sideways. Gus held onto the saddle horn, jammed his toe into the stirrup and pulled himself up.

Before he could get his leg over the saddle, Moriarty spun away.

Gus held onto the saddle horn, standing in the stirrup, waiting for the gelding to settle down enough to allow him to mount fully.

He cast a glance toward Daisy and Jane. The two stood a few feet away, calmly waiting for Gus to get Moriarty in check.

Out of the corner of his eye, Gus spied Franklin and Vasquez, grinning ear to ear over the amount of trouble Moriarty was giving Gus.

The competitive streak in Gus refused to back down. He pulled one of Moriarty's reins all the way to the right, making the horse spin in a circle until he came to a halt, his head hanging down.

Miss Daisy stood a few yards away, patiently watching what was happening with Moriarty and Gus.

She tossed her head at one point but stood still, waiting for her next command.

Thankfully, Jane wasn't pushing Daisy to do more than stand there and wait for Moriarty to get his shit together.

Finally, Gus was able to get his other leg over the horse's back and plant his foot in the stirrup. He reined the horse over to stand beside Daisy. Gus was fully in control, or as much in control as he could be with a horse that had a cantankerous personality. He'd thank Franklin and Vasquez later for their choice in his mount.

"What now?" Jane's hands gripped Daisy's reins, her fingers wrapping around the leather straps as naturally as breathing.

"You can make a few circles around the barnyard," Franklin suggested. "Unless you prefer a little more of a challenge."

"We prefer a challenge," Jane called out.

Gus cringed, wanting to tell Jane that she didn't know what she was getting into and that she should reconsider.

In the end, she had to make her own decision, which he was certain she hadn't been allowed to do for however long she'd been held captive.

"I'll get the gate." Vasquez walked past Gus and Jane.

By the time Gus wheeled his horse around, Vasquez had a gate open, not to the four-acre pasture, but to the thousand-acre range.

Before Gus could protest, Jane and Daisy flew through the open gate and raced across the field.

"Fuck."

Moriarty leaped forward and gave chase. The gelding liked to be first. In this instance, Gus was glad of the animal's bad habit. The sooner he caught up with Jane, the better. What was she thinking, tearing off like that?

Unless Daisy had gotten the bit between her teeth and was out of control.

Gus had no idea of Jane's skill level on a horse.

He didn't catch up to the mare until she slowed, running out of steam. By then, they were far from the house and barn.

Moriarty trotted up beside Daisy, tossing his head as if to scold the mare for showing off.

"Are you okay?" Gus asked.

Jane glanced over at him, her eyes wide, a grin

stretching across her face. "Better than okay. Nothing beats riding wild and free on the back of a horse with the wind in your hair."

Her face glowed with her joy.

Gus wanted to be angry at her for taking off like she had. Witnessing her happiness, he didn't have the heart to tell her off.

The horses settled into a swaying walk.

"You had me scared for a while there," Gus said. "I thought maybe Daisy had taken off with you."

Jane gave him a crooked smile. "Sorry. I couldn't hold back. I needed to fly."

Gus could only imagine the need to be free after being held captive. He'd probably feel the same. "You seem natural on a horse."

She swayed gracefully with the mare's movement. "I spent my summers riding a friend's horse. Mostly bareback. After my mother died, flying with the wind in my hair was the only time I could be me. No one judging or telling me I wasn't good enough. Just me, the horse and the sky."

"What happened to your mother?"

When Jane didn't answer immediately, Gus figured it was just one more secret she hadn't shared with anyone yet.

"Overdose," Jane said softly.

Since Gus hadn't expected an answer, he almost didn't hear the single whispered word.

"I'm sorry," he said. "What about your father?"

She snorted. "He never was a part of my life. My mother said he was a bull rider who worked the rodeo circuits. She thought she was in love. He was only in town for a week. To me, he was nothing more than a sperm donor."

"Did he know your mother was pregnant with his child?" Gus asked.

Jane nodded. "Mom told him as soon as she discovered she was pregnant. He accused her of trying to trick him into marrying her that the baby wasn't his, and he wasn't going to get dragged into supporting it. Mom never talked to him again."

"Sounds like an asshole," Gus said. "Your mother was better off without him."

"Being a single mother on the rez is a hard life," Jane said. "Mom did her best to raise me, but it wasn't easy. Jobs were scarce and didn't pay much. When she hurt her back at the hotel where she worked, they weren't happy that she took time off to recover. After she returned to work, she was still in pain and couldn't get the work done fast enough for them. They fired her. I came home from school and found her on the couch with an empty bottle of pain meds on the table beside her. I think she was tired of struggling and gave up." Jane stared off into the distance. "It was the first time I'd seen her without a worried frown creasing her forehead. My last impression of my mother was that she was finally at peace."

After listening to her story, Gus didn't know what to say, so he said nothing, riding along beside her.

"I don't know about you," she said, "but I could use some more of that wind in my hair." She nudged Daisy's sides.

The horse took off at a trot and slowly increased her speed to a canter.

Gus followed, holding Moriarty back to give Jane space to feel the wind and freedom of flying.

Her long black hair floated behind her as she leaned over Daisy's neck, urging her to go faster.

Before Gus realized what was happening, Daisy stopped so suddenly Jane flew over her neck and landed on the ground in front of the mare.

Daisy reared, whinnying loudly, then spun and raced back the way they'd come.

Gus urged Moriarty forward. "Jane?"

She lay on her back, staring up at the sky. "I'm okay," she said as if she couldn't push enough air past her vocal cords. "Just had the wind knocked out of me."

Gus swung off Moriarty. As soon as his boots hit the ground, the dry rattling sound made Gus freeze, and his gut tighten.

"I don't know what got into Daisy," Jane said as she tried to sit up.

"Don't move," Gus commanded.

"It's okay," Jane insisted. "Nothing's broken."

"Jane," he said, his voice firm. "Don't move a single muscle."

Jane frowned. "Why? What's wrong?" She lay on her back, her gaze darting left then right.

"Just remain perfectly still." He drew a deep breath and eased toward her, moving slowly and carefully placing each step.

When he was within six feet of the woman, he stared down at the ground.

Coiled and ready to strike was the biggest diamondback rattlesnake Gus had ever encountered.

Jane had its full attention.

She turned her head slowly to look at what Gus was staring at. "Holy shit," she swore softly. "Is that what I think it is?"

"If you think it's a rattlesnake, then yes," he said, trying to make light of the situation. "He's really interested in you. Unless you want a new piercing, I suggest you remain completely motionless."

"Not moving a single muscle," she promised. "What are you going to do?"

He glanced around, looking for a long stick he could use to redirect the creature away from Jane. Unfortunately, they were in a field, too far from the tree-lined creeks to retrieve a stick long and strong enough to do the job.

"God, I hate snakes," he muttered. Gus wished he had thought to bring his pistol. Not that he could shoot the snake when it was so close to Jane. He was a good shot, but the risks were too high. What if he missed or the bullet ricocheted and hit Jane? They could wait it out.

The snake's rattling grew louder. He seemed to be getting more irritated by the second.

"Is he moving this way, or is that me being paranoid?" Jane whispered.

The snake inched closer to Jane, bringing him within striking distance.

Damn.

It was now or never.

Gus sucked in a breath, shot forward, and, with his boot, swept the snake out of range.

As soon as it landed, the snake slithered away, disappearing into the grass.

Gus held out his hand to Jane.

"Wow," she said as she laid her hand in his and let him draw her to her feet and into his arms. She leaned into him, her hand on his chest, her body warm against his. "You could've been bitten."

"I doubt his fangs would have gone through my boots." He liked how she felt in his arms and wasn't in a hurry to move away. He held her loosely. If she wanted to step back, she could.

For a long moment, she remained still, her gaze on her hand spread across his chest. "Thank you," she said, "for saving me from the snake and for making me feel safe."

His arm around her waist tightened. "I promised to keep you safe," he said.

She nodded as she looked up into his eyes. "I didn't think I could ever feel safe again. Or that I could trust any man."

"I don't blame you," Gus said, brushing a strand of hair behind her ear. "You've been through hell."

She leaned her cheek into his palm. "I should've been more open to you and Hannah from the beginning. You've both been nothing but kind and helpful." She drew a deep breath and looked at her hand again, resting on his chest. "It's just that it's not only my life at stake here. There are other women who are being used like they used me. Women who've been abducted and drugged." Her brow furrowed.

Gus was overwhelmed with the sudden desire to kiss away the worry etched on Jane's forehead.

"I tried to escape once," she continued. "The man in charge caught me and swore that if I ever got away and reported them to the authorities, he'd kill the other women and disappear." She glanced up again. "So, you see, I had to disappear so that he would assume I'd wandered off into the woods and died. He would expect that if I lived, I would go straight to the nearest law enforcement agency and report what they're doing. Since none of the local or state agencies have been alerted, I hope he thinks I'm dead. Maybe it'll buy time for those women until I'm strong enough to go back and free them."

Gus stiffened. "You're not planning on going back, are you?"

She shivered. "It's the last thing in the world I want to do, but I can't walk away and leave the others trapped in that horrible situation. They'd be better off dead. I know that's how I felt and still feel." Her voice caught on what sounded like a sob.

"Why would you still want to be dead?" He set her at arm's length and stared into her face. "You've come so far and been through so much. Now, you're free."

Her lips twisted, and her brow pinched. "I'm physically free. I don't think I'll ever be free of what they did to me." She looked away, her cheeks flooding with color. "I'll never feel clean again or live a normal life."

Gus's eyebrows drew together. "Why not? You're still young and healthy, based on the doctor's report. You have everything to live for."

She lifted one shoulder and let it fall. "I always dreamed of finding someone special, getting married in a fairytale wedding and having three or four children. Despite my less than stellar childhood, or maybe because of it, I convinced myself I could do a better job raising a family."

"That's not just a dream," Gus said. "You can make it a reality."

Jane shook her head. "Even if my reproductive system isn't wrecked, I don't think I could find a man I could trust. Hell, I'd first have to find a man who could look past my history and see the woman I am inside." She pressed a hand to her chest and looked anywhere but into Gus's eyes. "Then there's the matter of intimacy. What man would go into a relationship knowing I won't give him the physical release he needs."

"The abuse you endured will take time to come to grip with."

"*Will* I come to grip with it?" her eyebrows rose in challenge. "Will there be a man who can accept me, knowing I've been used by dozens of men? How could he accept me when I can't accept myself? I'm dirty, tainted and untouchable."

"Stop." Gus's fingers dug gently into Jane's arms. "You're brave, beautiful, intelligent and worthy of love. You didn't ask for those things to happen to you. Any man who holds that against you or thinks less of you because of it isn't worth your time or heartache."

Jane raised a hand to Gus's cheek. "You're sweet."

He frowned. "And you don't believe a word I just said."

"It's a nice theory." She sighed. "My future isn't even my top priority. Freeing the others is." She stepped backward. "It's time I did something about it."

Gus's arms dropped to his sides, concern knotting his gut. "How do you propose to free the others? You can't do it alone."

"Well, I can't and won't involve law enforcement. I'm afraid to tell anyone I'm alive. If word gets back to them, they might pull the plug on their operation." She shook her head. "I'll have to sneak in somehow."

Gus didn't like the direction of her thoughts. "And if you're recaptured?"

Her jaw tightened. "I can't let that happen. I might be the only chance the others have."

Was she still loopy from the residual effects of the drugs? Gus shook his head. "You can't seriously think you can mount this freedom operation by yourself."

"I don't know what else to do," she said.

"You need help."

She paced a few steps away, turned and faced him. "Don't you see? I don't know who I can trust. These men have been running their operation for months without being caught. For all I know, they could have connections with people in law enforcement."

"You have to trust someone." Gus stepped closer. "Why not me?"

Her gaze swept over him.

"Have I done anything to hurt you?" he asked.

Her lips quirked.

His mouth twisted in a wry grin. "Besides dropping down on you from a haystack."

She stared at him hard before answering. "No."

"Let me help."

Jane frowned. "I don't want anyone else to be hurt."

"I'll take the risk."

Her frown deepened. "What's in it for you?"

"I've spent my adult life defending our country and the people in it while serving as a Navy SEAL. It's what I did and what I do now. Just because I'm not on active duty doesn't change who I am or what drives me. I'm a protector. The people I work with are the same. We're highly trained for combat as well as search and extraction. We can help. You don't have to do this on your own."

She chewed on her bottom lip. "I barely trust you...no offense."

He grinned. "But you do. And I'd trust the men of the Brotherhood Protectors with my life."

"That's all well and good. Your life isn't on the edge. If those women were your sisters, nieces or your mother, would you trust your brotherhood with their lives?"

Gus lifted his chin. "Absolutely. They can be trusted with lives and secrets. We have the added advantage of technical experts who can research and find just about anything on the internet or information buried in databases."

"Whatever I decide to do, it has to be soon," Jane said. "I'm afraid to wait any longer. Even if they don't kill those women, they could move further away and become harder to find."

"The team can mobilize quickly. We just have to say the word."

Her eyebrows knitted. "And you're certain they won't leak information to anyone outside your brotherhood?"

He held up his hand like he had when he'd sworn into the Navy. "I swear we can be trusted with secrets."

For a long moment, Jane studied him.

Gus prayed she'd allow him and his team to help her. He suspected that, even if Jane didn't agree to let them assist, they'd be all in to free the women once Stone Jacobs and Hank Patterson heard her story.

"You're right," she said. "I need help. This operation is too important to botch because I'm being stubborn or unrealistic." She lifted her chin and held out her hand. "Yes, please. Help me free those women."

He took her hand in his and covered it with his other. "And you'll tell us everything you know? We'll need as much information about the people and the setup as you can recall."

She grimaced. "I hope your people are really good at digging up information. I was drugged the entire time I was held in captivity. I'm not even sure if what I remember is real. I could've been hallucinating."

"Let's get you back to the ranch, contact my team and make it happen."

She nodded and glanced around. "That could take a while. Our horses seem to have ditched us."

Gus nodded. "It appears like it. Daisy will be back

at the barn by now. But as cantankerous as Moriarty is, he rarely strays too far from his rider." Gus curled his thumb and forefinger together and raised them to his lips. He blew air between the gap, emitting a sharp whistle.

An answering whinny sounded from over the top of a rise. Moments later, Moriarty galloped over that rise and came to stand in front of Gus.

"Good boy," he said.

"I've always wanted to learn how to whistle like that," Jane said.

"When the ladies are all safely freed, I'll teach you," he promised.

Jane grinned. "Deal."

Gus gathered Moriarty's reins and stood beside the horse. "Shall I drive or you?"

She nodded. "You drive. The stirrups are adjusted for you."

Gus mounted the gelding and reached for Jane's hand.

He had to pull her up enough for her to get her foot into the stirrup, then swung her around to sit behind the saddle on the horse's back.

"Hold on," he cautioned. "Moriarty doesn't ease into anything. It's all or nothing with him."

Jane's arms wrapped around Gus's waist. He smiled to himself. The woman had every reason never to want to touch a man again. Yet, she'd wrapped her arms around him and pressed her chest against his back without hesitation. Not that there was anything sexual going on between them.

He liked to think her willingness to hold onto him demonstrated a level of trust. Gus hoped he could maintain and build more trust with her.

She might not have any sexual thoughts about him, but Gus couldn't say the same for himself. Her breasts rubbing against his back and her hands wrapped around his waist ignited the blood in his veins. Not that he'd do anything about this burgeoning desire. Jane had a long way to go to recover from the abuse she'd endured. Gus didn't want to get in the way of that recovery.

Ready to nudge Moriarty to get him moving, Gus adjusted the reins in his hands.

"Gus?" Jane's words and breath warmed his shoulder blade.

"Yeah," he responded, holding Moriarty steady for another moment.

"My name isn't Jane."

He chuckled. "I didn't think it was."

"It's Peyton Running Bear," she said softly.

"Peyton," he repeated, rolling the name around on his tongue. "It suits you." Gus nudged Moriarty's flanks with his heels.

The gelding leaped forward.

Peyton's arms tightened around Gus's waist.

In that moment, Gus felt closer to this woman than he had since finding her behind the haystack.

And having her name was the first step in solving her problem.

After listening to her goal to free the others, Gus worried they might not find the women soon enough to save them. Without a doubt, Peyton would want to be in the thick of the rescue. Protecting the woman would be more of a challenge than initially anticipated.

He didn't care how difficult the task might be. Failure was not an option.

CHAPTER 11

NOW THAT PEYTON had taken that leap of faith and trust, some of the weight of responsibility eased from her shoulders. Instead of being paralyzed by the enormity of what she had to do, she felt optimistic that it could be done. That the women could be saved.

Being with Gus had also given her hope for some future sense of normalcy where men were concerned. Maybe not all of them were evil pigs with only one thing on their minds.

Gus hadn't once made a pass at her. He appeared to respect her as a person and didn't seem disgusted by the truth of what had happened to her.

She was surprised at how safe she felt with him and how being with Gus made her feel like she wasn't completely alone.

His words and actions held no hint of judgment or worse...pity.

With her arms wrapped around his taut belly, her chest and cheek pressed against his back, she didn't want the ride to end. She loved flying solo on a horse. However, flying with Gus was even better.

The man was an island in the river that had been raging around her. He'd saved her from drowning, and now, he'd help her save the others.

When they arrived at the barn, Franklin, Vasquez, Taz and Hannah met them, worried frowns denting their brows.

"We were just about to go looking for you," Hannah said.

Taz nodded. "When Daisy arrived back at the barn without her rider, we figured something happened."

"What happened?" Franklin asked.

Gus turned in the saddle. "It's your story. Do you want to tell it?" He offered Peyton his arm.

Peyton held onto his arm as she slid off the horse and dropped to the ground. "You tell it," she said. "You were the hero."

The corners of his lips quirked upward. "Far from it. I was terrified."

Peyton rolled her eyes. "Whatever." She turned to Hannah and gave her the short version. "Daisy got spooked by a snake, dumped me on the ground beside said snake and took off. Gus got rid of the snake and brought me back. The end."

Vasquez and Franklin's eyebrows shot up.

"Gus wrangled a snake?" Vasquez asked.

"More like shooed it away," Gus offered. "Or, to be more precise, I booted it away." He dismounted and started to lead Moriarty into the barn.

"Let someone else take the horse." Taz tipped his head toward the ranch house. "You need to make a phone call. Hank Patterson has been trying to contact you."

"I'll take care of him," Franklin said.

"And Daisy?" Peyton asked.

"Already taken care of," Vasquez said. "She's munching sweet feed in the stall beside Lady. I think Lady likes the company."

Gus met Peyton's gaze. "Ready?"

She gave him an almost imperceptible nod. Yes, she was still on board with bringing the Brotherhood Protectors in on the daring rescue mission. Like Gus had pointed out, his team had experience with this kind of operation.

Telling Gus the details would be easy. He'd proven himself safe and reliable. Peyton knew little about his team of protectors. She prayed they were as loyal and trustworthy as Gus.

"I can set you up on a video conference call in the office," Taz said. He led the way to the ranch house and into the office, where a large desk occupied one end of the room and a small conference table took up the other side. A large screen hung on the wall at the end of the conference table.

Gus held a chair as Peyton took a seat at the table. Then he slid into the chair beside her, his thigh brushing against hers.

That closeness gave her a little sense of comfort, grounding her when she felt like she was teetering on the edge of a precipice about to leap off.

Taz's fingers flew across a computer keyboard. After a couple of minutes, he placed a video call. An image of a dark-haired man appeared on the big screen.

"Oh, good, you found them." The man nodded toward Peyton and Gus. "You must be Jane."

Peyton drew in a breath and jumped in. "Actually, my name is Peyton."

Hank nodded solemnly. "Nice to meet you, Peyton. Glad you're getting around better today."

She let go of the breath she'd held. "Gus tells me your Brotherhood Protectors might be able to help me."

Hank dipped his head. "That's what we do. And that's why I called. I wanted to give you an update."

Gus reached for Peyton's hand.

She laid hers in his.

"Swede and Kyla combed through the surveillance

videos at the truck stop where Hannah and Taz acquired their extra passenger." He smiled gently at Peyton. "After careful scrutiny, they were able to find brief images of a small person we assume was you, moving through the parking lot. They traced that person back to where she slipped out of the back of a red and white, older model pickup. We backed up the video further before you left the truck. Once we knew what we were looking for, we followed you from where you left the pickup. You moved from the regular parking lot to the lot where the bigger vehicles parked, including Hannah's truck and horse trailer."

"Did you get a license plate on the truck she arrived in?" Gus asked.

Hank gave a single nod. "We couldn't get an image of the plate where the truck was parked. Swede and Kyla fast-forwarded an hour and reviewed several different camera angles before they found one that recorded the truck leaving the lot. We captured a partial plate number and ran it against the Montana DMV database."

Peyton leaned forward. "Whose truck was it?"

"The truck belonged to a Roy Blanchard," Hank said. "Swede ran a search on the man. He works for a ranch near the border between Montana and Wyoming."

"Thus, the stop in Livingston," Taz concluded.

"Roy was one of the customers," Peyton said quietly. "I remember hearing his buddy call out his name."

"In that case, he should know where the trailers are parked," Hank said.

Peyton shook her head. "Not necessarily. They move the trailers every night to keep unwanted people from finding them."

"How do their customers find them?" Hank asked.

"I don't know. They came in waves." She closed her eyes, trying to remember events she'd rather forget. "It was like they followed events where a lot of men were celebrating...? They kept us so drugged that it's all hazy. I don't know if I'm remembering real events or nightmares my imagination conjured."

"Probably both," Hannah stared at Peyton from her seat across the table.

"What ranch does Roy work for?" Gus asked.

"He works at the K-BAR-M Ranch. It's a large cattle operation with over one hundred thousand acres. They employ twenty-seven people. Roy is one of them. I suspect the man who was with him in the truck works there as well."

"Jim," Peyton blurted. "Roy called the other man Jim if that helps."

Hank turned away from the camera. "Did you hear that, Swede?"

A voice sounded in the background.

Hank returned his attention to the camera. "Swede says there are a couple of men named James on the payroll at the K-Bar-M. He also pulled a rap sheet on Roy. The man had a couple of domestic disturbances, aggravated assault and public intoxication."

"We need to talk to him," Gus said.

"I sent one of my guys south as soon as we identified Roy as one of the customers," Hank said.

Peyton's pulse raced. "He's not going to mention me, is he?"

Hank gave her a reassuring smile. "No. He's going in undercover as a ranch hand with the Double Diamond Ranch out of Colorado. He's in Livingston for a horse auction that's taking place as we speak. We set him up in an Airbnb across the street from Roy's place."

Peyton sat back in her chair, willing her pulse to slow.

"Our guy will observe the man, follow him to his favorite bar and buy him some drinks." Hank's eyes narrowed.

"He was falling down drunk the last time I...saw him," Peyton said. "Shouldn't be hard to get him talking."

Hank nodded. "That's the idea. And when he's had enough to loosen his tongue, our guy will ask where he can find some female entertainment."

"Who'd you tap for the job?" Taz asked.

"Kujo," Hank responded.

Peyton frowned. "Kujo?"

"Kuntz, Joseph. Kujo," Hank explained. "He's good at what he does."

"He won't mention me?" Peyton asked, her anxiety spiking.

"Everyone who will be involved in this case will be under strict orders to refrain from mentioning the name Peyton Running Bear," Hank said.

Peyton gasped, her heart sinking to the pit of her belly. "I only told you my first name. How..."

Hank stared through the screen directly at Peyton. "Because of where you were the night you stowed away on Hannah's horse trailer, we made an educated guess that you were from the Wind River Reservation. Swede ran a query on the national missing persons database, narrowing the search to women fitting your description who'd disappeared from Wind River. We found your aunt's report and compared the image she'd submitted with the one Gus sent, and *bingo*." Hank smiled. "Peyton Running Bear."

Her lips pressed together. She shot a narrowed glance at Gus. "What picture did you send?"

"I snapped one with my cell phone." Gus had the decency to flush a ruddy red. "You were asleep. Otherwise, I would've asked."

The fact he'd taken the picture without telling her hit her square in her trust.

She returned her gaze to Hank. "What else did you find out about me?"

"The missing person report had notes from your aunt and the tribal police. Your aunt filed the initial report. The tribal police added that your vehicle was found abandoned on the side of the road with a flat tire. Their investigation discovered a screwdriver sticking out of the inside of the right front tire. You were last seen by your manager at the convenience store where you worked."

Flashbacks of that night flooded into Peyton's mind. She'd just gotten out of her car and discovered the flat tire. Headlights blinded her as a van pulled up behind her vehicle. At first, she'd been glad someone had come along, hopefully, to help her change the tire. She'd only done it once herself, and that had been in the daylight.

When three men emerged from the van, she'd immediately sensed that they weren't there to help her. She'd tried to get back into her car, but they were on her before she could open the door.

One man had grabbed her from behind, trapping her arms to her sides. The other had jabbed a needle into her arm. As the drug had entered her bloodstream, her vision blurred, but not before she saw the man she would come to know as Snake nod and say,

"She'll be a good replacement for Lola. Just don't screw up the dosage this time."

Then, as if trapped in a horror movie, she'd been carried to the van, where they'd zip-tied her wrists and ankles and left her lying on the cold metal floor. She hadn't been able to fight, to run or even scream. As they'd driven away from her car, she'd known her life would never be the same again.

Peyton's pulse raced, slamming blood through her veins. She could feel the thunder of her heartbeat pounding against her eardrums. Her breathing became so erratic that she couldn't fill her lungs. Her head spun, and her heart pinched painfully in her chest.

Peyton pushed back from the table and leaped to her feet, the sudden urge to run so intense she had to move or lose her shit.

She whipped around so fast her head swam, her vision blurred, and she stumbled.

Gus was beside her, his arm circling her waist, catching her before she fell. He gently pulled her into his arms in a featherlight hold she could easily break. She leaned into him, grateful for his solid strength and ability to reach her quickly.

"Breathe, Peyton," he murmured against her ear.

She tried, but her breaths were tiny gasps, bringing little oxygen to her lungs.

Gus gripped her arms and set her at arm's length, staring intently into her eyes. "Look at me, Peyton."

She met his gaze and held it like a life preserver in a stormy sea. Everything else, everyone in the room, faded into the background.

In his deep, calm tone, he said, "Take a deep breath with me." Gus drew in a long, steady breath.

Peyton focused on Gus, breathing in like he did.

"Now, let it out slowly," he said, releasing his breath a little at a time.

Peyton did the same.

"Again," Gus said softly, sucking in a deep breath that Peyton copied.

And they let out the air at the same time.

One more round of deep breathing and Peyton's pulse slowed, the pounding in her ears subsided and the pain in her chest eased.

"One more time?" Gus asked.

Peyton shook her head. "No. I've got it from here." When she finally broke away from his gaze, she looked around the room. All eyes were on her.

Heat rose in her cheeks. "I'm sorry," she said and sank into her chair, wishing she could sink into the floor.

"Don't be," Hannah said.

"I don't know what got into me," Peyton murmured.

"Did your heart race to the point you felt like you were having a heart attack," Gus asked.

Peyton pressed a hand to her chest, the ache there having dissipated. "Yes."

"You had a panic attack," Hannah said. "It's all part of Post-Traumatic Stress."

"I thought only guys who'd been at war got PTSD," Peyton said.

"What you went through was as traumatic as what they've been through," Hannah said. "People who've been in violent or abusive situations can have PTSD."

"Great." Peyton snorted. "I shouldn't have been so eager for the drugs to clear my system."

"If it makes you feel any better," Gus said. "I came to Brighter Days to get help managing my PTSD. Hannah works miracles."

Peyton frowned up at Gus. "You have panic attacks?"

He nodded. "They don't happen as often now as they did."

"Peyton," Hank said, drawing attention to the big screen. "You're in the right place with the right people. Work with Hannah; she's an excellent therapist. She'll help you through recovery."

Peyton shook her head, her hands clenching into fists. "I don't have time for panic attacks, therapy or recovery. I wasn't the only woman trapped in that hell. I have to do something to get them out of it. Spontaneously falling apart is not an option."

A smile played at the corners of Hank Patterson's mouth. "Right. Falling apart is not an option. You've come this far; you *will* see it through. And we'll be with you all the way." He gave her a nod. "I've told you what I know. Tell us everything you can remember. Names and descriptions of people, places, vehicles, anything, no matter how insignificant it might seem."

PEYTON SQUARED her shoulders and prayed that what little she remembered would be enough.

CHAPTER 12

PEYTON TOOK a deep breath and forced herself to step back into what memories she could recall through the drug-induced haze she'd existed in for the past months.

"The man in charge of the trailers, the women and the men who served as guards, keepers and drivers was called Snake." She shook her head. "I never heard anyone call him by any other name. I know that's not very helpful."

"What did he look like?" Hank asked.

Peyton squeezed her eyes shut, her thoughts going back to her first encounter with the man. "He has dark hair, dark eyes and a goatee." She remembered the eyes being almost black and completely void of emotion. "He's not as tall as the other guys, but he's not exactly short. It seemed like everything he wore was black. Black jeans, black T-shirts, a black jacket with a hood. He keeps his keys attached to a silver chain hooked to his belt loop, with the keys tucked into his pocket. He rattles them when he's angry."

"Does he have any scars, tattoos or piercings?" Gus asked.

"He has a scar on his lip that makes him look like he's sneering all the time." She thought back over every confrontation she'd had with the man, her mind replaying the scenes. The time she'd first attempted to escape, Snake had been so angry he'd pushed up his sleeves and punched her in the gut. He'd always been careful not to damage the faces of his "products," as he referred to the women. Their faces were the first thing his clients saw.

It was when he'd pushed up his sleeve that she'd noticed a tattoo on his forearm. What was it? She pinched the bridge of her nose and tried to adjust the focus on her memory.

At first, she'd assumed it was a snake with a long, swirling tail, but the head wasn't right. The head had a square snout and horns. "A dragon," she said, opening her eyes. "He has a dragon on his right forearm."

She described the three camp trailers they'd moved from site to site, setting up shop where they had a paying audience.

"Do you remember the colors, makes or models of the trailers," Hank asked.

She shook her head. "We were rarely allowed outside. I only remember that they were covered in dust. One had large letters on the front. I thought it odd that it spelled out the name of a Native American people. I'm Arapaho. It wasn't Arapaho or Shoshone."

"Apache?" Taz suggested.

Peyton shook her head. The letters were there in her mind, but not clear.

"Sioux?" Gus offered. "Cheyenne?"

"Navajo?" Hannah said. "Cherokee?"

"Cherokee!" Peyton said, pleased she'd dragged that small detail out of her cloudy memory.

She went on to describe the other men who'd fed and drugged them.

"Were your captors Caucasian?" Hank asked.

Peyton frowned. "Snake was. But, the group is a mix of Caucasians and Native Americans. I remember feeling betrayed by people who might even belong to my tribe."

"What about the clients?" Hank asked, his tone matter-of-fact and non-judgmental.

They'd been a blur of men. Short, tall, thin, heavy, hairy and bald.

"A lot of cowboys," she said.

"And you know that because...?" Hank prompted.

"Boots, jeans, hats, smell..." she scrunched her eyes, thinking, "and big, shiny belt buckles. I remember the belt buckles because they were the only things that stood out in the darkened haze. It was dark even in the daytime. The windows were blacked out, and half the light bulbs were burned out."

"What did they use to tow the trailers?" Taz asked.

"White trucks," she said.

"Any writing on the sides?" Hank prompted.

She shook her head. "One had a dent in the driver's side rear panel. I only noticed it because the taillight was busted out and covered with red duct tape."

Peyton racked her brain for anything else that might help. "I'm sorry I don't have more information than that."

"It's okay," Hank said. "We have our team working on this. I'll let you know what we find. If you think of anything else—"

"I'll let you know," Peyton promised. "And, in the meantime?"

"Rest and get your strength back," Hank said.

Peyton shook her head. "I keep thinking about those other women. There should be more that I can do to help."

"You're already helping," Hannah said. "You could've walked away and never looked back. But you chose to do something about their situation."

"The Brotherhood Protectors are committed to this mission," Hank said. "We'll do our very best to free those women and put an end to that operation."

Peyton slipped her hand into Gus's. "That's all I

can ask. Thank you, Hank. I look forward to hearing from you."

"Out here," Hank said. A moment later, the screen went blank.

Peyton rose with the others and left the office.

Hannah headed to the kitchen. "I need to check with Cookie about this evening's meal."

Taz left, muttering something about fixing the clutch on a tractor.

Peyton walked out of the house onto the wide back porch.

"What are your plans for the rest of the afternoon?" Gus asked.

She stared out at the fields and the mountains, physically and emotionally exhausted. But she couldn't relax knowing she was free, but the others were still trapped. "I can't stand around doing nothing."

"And we can't just stab in the dark," Gus said. "We have to have a lead to follow. Hopefully, Kujo will learn something in Livingston."

"Would it help if we were there as well?" Peyton asked.

"You said yourself that you can't be seen."

She nodded. "Snake's threat. What if I wear a disguise?"

"Let's see what Kujo comes up with tonight," Gus said. "That'll give you another day to recuperate."

"And if he doesn't learn anything new? I'm not

convinced Roy knows where the trailers will be next. Snake wasn't pleased with him. He might not invite him to come back."

"Hank will have briefed Kujo about Roy's buddy, Jim. If he doesn't get anything out of Roy, he'll find Jim. Give him until tomorrow. If we don't have anything to go on, we'll try something else. In the meantime, if you don't want to rest, relax or read a book, how about working with the horses?"

Peyton frowned, finding it hard to focus on anything when the lives of others hung in the balance. Then she thought of Lady.

"Good idea," Peyton said. "I think better when I'm brushing a horse, and I know just the horse."

She marched out to the barn with Gus on her heels. She paused at the stall where Daisy munched on hay. The mare pressed her nose into Peyton's hand, allowing her to stroke her soft muzzle. "So, you and Gus have something in common," she said softly.

"We both hate snakes," Gus said.

"At least you didn't run away like this big baby," Peyton said.

Gus chuckled. "The thought crossed my mind."

Peyton smiled up at him. "But you didn't." She moved to the next stall, where Lady stood in the back corner.

"Hey, girl, did they find a friend to keep you company?" Peyton crooned to the poor animal. She looked over her shoulder at Gus. "You can leave me here with Lady. We have some girl-talk to catch up on."

Gus gave her a crooked smile. "I guess I could muck a stall or polish some saddles." His brow wrinkled. "Girl-talk, huh?"

"I told you," Peyton said. "I think better when I'm brushing a horse."

"Hold that thought." Gus spun, retraced his steps and ducked into the tack room. A moment later, he emerged, carrying a brush and a curry comb. "You might need these to help you think."

Peyton took the offerings, leaned up on her toes and brushed a kiss across his cheek. "Thank you."

Then she dove into the stall and closed the gate behind her.

What the hell had she just done?

Her lips tingled from their contact with Gus's cheek and the beginnings of his five o'clock shadow.

Peyton's stomach fluttered with what felt like a thousand butterflies. How could she even consider kissing a man after everything she'd been through?

With her back to the gate, she refused to look over her shoulder in case Gus was still standing there.

He probably thought nothing of the insignificant little kiss she'd given him.

In Peyton's current world, the kiss, given without thinking, meant a lot more than a thank you. It meant she had a chance at rebuilding her life.

Don't overthink it, she schooled herself.

Concentrate on how to find Snake and the trailers.

She spent the next hour brushing Lady, working through the knots in her mane and tail and applying medicine to her sores.

When she was done, she was no closer to coming up with another plan than when she'd started grooming Lady.

At least she was calm, relaxed and happy for Lady. With plenty of food to eat and a warm stall, the horse was beginning to perk up.

As Peyton and Gus left the barn to clean up for dinner, something tugged at the back of Peyton's mind. She'd gone over everything she could remember from the moment she'd been abducted to arriving at Brighter Days Rehab Ranch.

What was she missing?

She stopped trying to force the thought from her head and focused on the fact that a lot of people on the rehab ranch now knew her name. They'd sworn to keep her secret. What made keeping the secret hard were the other guests living there. It would be too easy for someone to forget for a moment and call her by her real name.

As she and Gus climbed the porch steps, Peyton stopped short of the door. "Given my desire to remain as anonymous as possible. I think eating dinner in my room might be easier for everyone. Do you think Cookie would mind if I took a plate upstairs?"

"Not at all," Gus opened the door and held it for her. "In fact, if you don't mind, I'll join you."

She smiled at him, suddenly shy with this man who took to heart keeping her safe. "I'd like that."

They entered the kitchen as Cookie was sprinkling paprika on a bowl of potato salad. "You're early," he said.

Peyton smiled at the ranch chef. "Everything smells so good." She sighed. "I'm sorry, but I don't think I have the energy to socialize. I think I'll just go upstairs, shower and go straight to bed."

Cookie's eyes widened. "You can't go to bed without supper." He turned, fished a tray from a cabinet and plunked a plate on it. "It'll only take me a minute to make a plate for you."

Gus chuckled. "I'm joining Ms. Black for her private dinner."

"Grab a tray and help yourself," Cookie said as he loaded Peyton's plate with a pork chop, potato salad and green beans. He added a slice of apple pie to the tray. "There are sodas in the refrigerator, or you can snag one of those single-serving bottles of wine from the pantry."

Peyton started for the refrigerator, altered course for the pantry and grabbed one of the little bottles of red wine.

When she emerged, Gus was adding a beer to his loaded tray.

Cookie held Peyton's tray out in front of him. "Lead the way. I've got your tray."

"I can carry it," she said.

Cookie shook his head. "Let me do this. I haven't lost a plate in sixty-three days. I'm trying to beat my previous record of one hundred and five days."

"I promise I won't drop the tray," Peyton said. Her protests fell on deaf ears.

Cookie was already out of the kitchen and halfway to the staircase.

Peyton had to hurry to keep up.

Gus followed, chuckling. "Cookie's serious about his dinnerware."

By the time Peyton reached her room, Cookie had set the tray on the table beside the chair. He passed her, going out as she was coming in. "Bon appétit!"

Gus set his tray on the yellow comforter. "I'll be right back." He darted out the door. Moments later, he returned carrying a desk chair and set it beside the floral chair near the French doors.

He adjusted the side table, moving it closer so that Peyton could reach her plate. Then he opened her bottle of wine and poured it into the glass Cookie had provided.

"Thank you," she said, pleased at his attention to detail and his attention to her. She'd never met a man who'd treated her so well. Probably because she was his client. The mission. His job.

Regardless of why he did all those things for her, she was grateful.

He settled in the desk chair with his tray across his lap and popped the tab on his can of beer. "To kicking ass and saving lives," he said and lifted his drink.

She raised her wine glass. "Here! Here!"

For the next few minutes, they ate in silence.

Peyton savored every bite of the tender porkchop and potato salad. Even the green beans were delicious. By the time she got to the apple pie, she had to stop and breathe a second. "Cookie is an amazing chef."

"He's so good it's hard to get the guests to leave once they're deemed ready to face the world." He raised his beer. "I'm a prime example. Hannah had given me my marching orders the day you arrived. I wasn't looking forward to packing up and leaving Cookie's great food."

"Her therapy really helped you?" Peyton dug her fork into the flaky crust of the slice of apple pie.

"She helped a lot."

"And you have PTSD?"

"As much as I hated admitting it, yes. The nightmares and panic attacks were impacting my health. I didn't want to go to sleep because I knew I'd have the same nightmare over and over. Sleep deprivation made me a zombie, barely able to function."

Peyton took a bite of apple pie and chewed, studying the man in the chair beside her. He looked healthy and rested. "You'd never know you were once a zombie," she said.

"Hannah helped me come to terms with the past." He set down his beer and dug his fork into his pie. "She taught me techniques for managing panic attacks and gave me hope for a healthy future."

"So, she gave you marching orders?" Peyton frowned. "Does that mean you're cured?"

He laughed. "Hardly. But I'm learning to accept what I can't change, and I have the tools I need to get me through the day. The most important lesson I've learned is that if I want to be happy, I have to choose to be happy. No one else can do that for me."

Peyton sighed. "I guess I have my work cut out for me to get to the point where you are."

"You'll get there." Gus finished his pie. "Are you done with your dinner?"

Peyton nodded. "It was amazing."

Gus stacked the plates and trays together. "Did you need anything from the kitchen?"

She shook her head. "No. I think I'll get my shower and call it a night."

Gus nodded. "Goodnight, Peyton. We're going to figure this out."

She gave him a weak smile. "I truly hope so."

If they didn't figure it out soon, those women could die.

After he left, Peyton stripped out of her dirty clothes, showered and pulled on the nightgown Sadie had sent. She'd never had such a beautiful garment to sleep in. The satiny, smooth material glided over her skin like air, caressing every curve.

She brushed the tangles from her hair, smoothing it straight back from her forehead, the damp tresses cool against her back.

On the surface, she looked like any other sexy and desirable woman. It was what was inside that made her doubt herself. Who could love a woman like her?

A soft knock sounded on the door.

"Peyton, are you awake?" Gus's voice sounded from the other side.

Heat rushed through her body. "Y-yes," she answered.

"Can I come in?"

Her gaze shot around the room for something she could throw on to cover her body in the silky soft gown. She found a throw blanket draped over the end of the iron bed, wrapped it around her shoulders and hurried to open the door.

He grinned. "You were fast in the shower. I wanted to show you something before you go to sleep." He stepped past her, crossed to the wall on the right and pushed a small dresser several feet over, revealing a door Peyton hadn't noticed before.

"It's a connecting door between our rooms." He twisted the lock on the doorknob and turned the handle. When Gus opened the door, Peyton could see into the room on the other side.

Where her room was filled with yellow sunshine colors, his was a smoky blue with simple wood furniture and photographs of colorful pheasants and mallard ducks.

"I'm leaving my side unlocked. You can choose to lock yours...or not. I just wanted to let you know you had options. Either way, all you have to do is yell, and I'll find a way through. Last night, Hannah and I alternated staying with you, afraid you'd try to get up on your own and then fall and hurt yourself."

Peyton frowned. "You did?"

He nodded.

If they'd taken turns, they'd had to go in and out of her room. "How did I not know this?"

He grinned. "You slept like you hadn't slept for a long time."

Her cheeks heated. "Well, thanks for looking out for me. You don't have to worry about me falling tonight. I think I'm pretty steady on my feet now."

"Yes, you are," Gus gave her a brief nod. "Good night, J-Peyton." He grinned. "I'm still getting used to calling you Peyton." He stared down at her, his blue eyes open and friendly. So different from the darkness and evil of Snake's black eyes. "Peyton suits you more than Jane."

"How so?"

The blue in his eyes turned smoky as his gaze swept over her face. "It's like you, intelligent, mysterious and beautiful." His voice had deepened, the resonance washing over her like warm summer air on naked skin.

Heat coiled at her center and spread throughout her body. For a long moment, she stood transfixed by his gaze, wrapped in the embrace of his words.

Gus blinked, breaking the spell. He touched a finger to her cheek and smiled. "Sleep well, Peyton Running Bear. If you wake at night and need me for any reason, I'm on the other side of the door." He stepped through and pulled the door halfway closed. "Your choice," he reminded her and drifted out of sight.

"I choose you," she whispered without thinking. When she realized what she'd said, she slapped a hand over her mouth.

What was she thinking? There was no choosing Gus. He was there to protect her, not make love to her.

Sweet Jesus, had he heard her?

She stood perfectly still, listening for sounds of his laughter because, surely, he'd laugh if he'd heard her say those words.

Peyton reached for the door, fully intending to close and lock it. Gus needed to know she had no intention of pursuing a romantic relationship with him. He deserved a woman with a lot less...history. A beautiful, wholesome woman who wouldn't flinch when he touched her. One who could bear his children.

The doctor in the emergency room had checked her for STDs, which, thankfully, she was clear of. But he hadn't been a gynecologist. For that matter, could a specialist tell by looking if the abuse she'd endured had ruined her ability to have children?

Her eyes burned. What if she couldn't have children?

Her dream of having kids had hinged on her finishing college and getting a job that paid enough money to support herself and any children she might have.

She'd been halfway through her last semester of prerequisites and had applied to the nursing program at Montana State University in Bozeman.

Had her instructors wondered what had happened to her? Had she received an acceptance letter to the nursing program? Would they rescind her acceptance because she hadn't completed her prerequisites as anticipated?

Did any of it matter? Would anyone even give a damn? No one had cared enough about her or the other women to come to their rescue.

She'd had to rescue herself. Now, she stood frozen at the door between her and a man she found attractive. Frozen in fear that she wasn't good enough, clean enough, pure enough.

She wasn't enough.

Why was she afraid? Hadn't she shown how brave she could be by daring to run into the night half-naked and barefoot to escape the hell of her captivity? She'd done it and survived.

Only to be paralyzed with the fear that she wasn't enough.

Her hand pushed the door slowly closed, only to stop a moment later, anger surging through her.

It was just a damned door, not a life-altering testimony to her courage.

Peyton pulled the door open wide.

Gus had turned out the lights in his room.

For a moment, Peyton stood in the doorway, unsure of what she'd just accomplished. Then she let the blanket drop from around her shoulders, fully aware that the light behind her would silhouette her body in the figure-hugging nightgown.

"Goodnight, Gus," she said.

"Goodnight, Peyton."

With her head held high, Peyton walked to her bed and lay on top of the bright comforter, adrenaline coursing through her veins. Too wound up to sleep, her mind too occupied with the man in the room a few steps away, she tried to concentrate on that niggling thought that she was missing something.

"Peyton?" Gus interrupted her non-productive thinking.

"Yeah," she answered.

"I spoke briefly with Hank when I took our trays down. I asked if Swede thought to tap into the surveillance videos at the convenience store where you worked."

"He couldn't if he wanted to," Peyton said. "The owner refuses to link his business to the internet."

"Does he have a surveillance system?" Gus asked.

"Yes, but it's not the greatest. He has a camera in front of the store, one in the back and another aimed at the cash register inside. They feed into the computer in his office. I know that because he made a big deal about it when he hired me. He said the last guy he'd fired had been stealing from him. He was only able to prove it when he'd installed the cameras."

"Do you think he'd let us review the videos?" Gus asked.

Peyton thought about her old boss. The man was as tight with his money as he was with his privacy and a huge gossip. "He never allowed employees in his office. He discouraged employees from standing around talking to family members, boyfriends or girlfriends on company time. Allow someone into the inner sanctum of his office? No. I don't think he'd let you in to review the videos."

"If he won't let me in," Gus said from his room, "is there a way we could get in anyway?"

Peyton grinned. "Yes. I hid a spare key to the store in the light fixture over the back entrance. I got tired of the back door closing and locking automatically when I took out the trash. I'd have to go to the front of the building to get back in."

"Does he keep the store open all night?" Gus asked.

Peyton snorted. "No. My boss used to keep it open twenty-four-seven. After the store was robbed twice, my boss started closing at midnight and opening at six o'clock in the morning."

"It's nine o'clock now," Gus said. "It takes a little over five hours to get to that store on Wind River Reservation." He appeared in the frame of the connecting door, wearing only a pair of gym shorts.

The air evaporated from Peyton's lungs as her gaze consumed Gus's broad naked chest and lowered to his narrow waist and hips to his thickly muscled thighs.

Peyton's pulse fluttered, and she had to swallow twice before she could push air past her vocal cords. "What are you suggesting?" She could think of a few things they could do that didn't involve breaking and entering into a convenience store.

But was it really breaking and entering if they had the key?

Gus met her gaze across the room. "If we get there just after two a.m., we'll have nearly three hours to review the videos." His brow furrowed. "That is if you know how to get into his computer."

A grin spread across Peyton's face. "I do. It's the same code he uses to log into the point-of-sale system at the cash register. I inadvertently caught him entering it as I waited for him to finish what he was doing before I interrupted." Peyton left the bed. "I can be ready in two minutes."

"Make it five and pack to stay in West Yellowstone when we're done in Wind River." He turned back to his room, tossed a suitcase onto the bed and tossed his belongings in.

Since she didn't have a suitcase, Peyton stacked all her new-to-her clothes neatly on the bed. She unfolded a long-sleeved blue chambray shirt, stretched it out on the bed, laid her stack of clothes in the middle and tied the long sleeves to secure the bundle.

Peyton grabbed a pair of black leggings, a black, long-sleeve cable-knit sweater and a bra and ducked into the bathroom to change out of the sexy nightgown.

She sighed as she dressed all in black and pulled her hair back. Making a second bundle, she filled it with clothing items, spare shoes, undergarments and the toiletries Hannah had provided. After she secured the items by wrapping up everything with a long-sleeve blouse, she turned toward the connecting door.

Gus strode through, wheeling a suitcase and carrying a large green duffel bag. "Ready?"

She nodded. Tired of waiting for something to happen, she embraced the idea of making it happen. Was she ready?

"Hell, yeah."

CHAPTER 13

WHEN THEY'D ARRIVED at the outskirts of Riverton, Wyoming, Gus had stopped a tenth of a mile short of their destination and parked his truck behind a rusted shipping container. From there, they'd walked the rest of the way to the convenience store on the edge of Riverton, careful to stay outside the range of any surveillance cameras.

Gus spent fifteen minutes studying the convenience store and the positions of the external cameras of the buildings on either side and across the street. The surrounding structures were boarded up and didn't pose a threat.

"We can avoid the front camera altogether," he told Peyton. "We need to shroud the back camera before we attempt to breach the back door."

Peyton held up a towel she'd pilfered from the

bathroom before she'd left Brighter Days. "Will this work?"

Gus grinned. "Absolutely. We'll approach from the side of the building. I'll lift you high enough so that you can drape the towel over the camera. Once it's blacked out, we can work on the back door."

"If the spare key is still where I left it in the light fixture," Peyton said, "we'll be inside in seconds."

Gus glanced at the illuminated dial on his watch. "It's a little past two o'clock now. We have less than three hours to get in, power up the computer and review the videos."

"Let's go," Peyton said.

They approached from the west side of the building and eased up to the corner. Gus wrapped his hands around Peyton's narrow waist. "Ready?"

She nodded.

He lifted her high enough she easily draped the towel over the light.

With the camera blocked, they moved quickly to the back door.

Peyton reached up to the light fixture, felt inside for the ledge and stilled.

"No key?" Gus asked.

She withdrew her hand from the light's housing and held up a key. Peyton pulled a napkin out of her pocket from their short stop at a gas station on their way south to the reservation. After wrapping the napkin around the back door handle, she fit the key into the lock and twisted it. The door opened, and Peyton stepped inside.

Gus released the breath he hadn't known he was holding and followed. Once through the door, he closed it behind him and twisted the deadbolt. They didn't need some drunk bumbling into the building because they hadn't thought to secure the lock.

Peyton shot ahead, stopping at a closed door. She wrapped the napkin around the knob and tried to open the door, but it was locked. "He wouldn't use the same key for this room, would he?" she murmured. She slipped the key into the lock and turned. Peyton grinned. "The man is a creature of habit. Do you want to drive, or shall I?"

"You're more familiar with the system here than I am," Gus said.

Peyton dropped into the battered office chair with its peeling vinyl fabric and laid the napkin she'd carried with her onto the mouse. As soon as she touched the mouse, a screen saver popped up with a login box at its center.

Peyton keyed the password she said she'd remembered Ned using and pressed ENTER. The screen churned for half a minute, blinked and displayed the home screen with a selection of icons. "We're in."

Gus found a folding chair leaning against the wall, unfolded it and sat beside Peyton as she navigated the system. She quickly located the surveillance application and scrolled back a few months to the date she'd been abducted.

Gus kept looking over his shoulder, half-expecting Ned Little Foot to walk in. At two-thirty in the morning, that possibility was highly unlikely.

When Peyton finally located the file from the day she'd been abducted, Gus leaned closer.

"What exactly are we looking for?" Peyton asked.

"Anything that stands out as not normal," Gus said.

Peyton played the video from the moment she'd arrived at work and parked her car on the far end of the front parking lot. Ned had insisted they leave prime spots for customers.

Fast forwarding a little at a time, Peyton ran through the hours, quickly working up to the time she'd left work.

The front camera picked up almost everything happening in the parking lot, though it was a little hazy with the distance to the point where Peyton had parked her car.

An hour before she'd left her shift, several customers entered the store. The interior camera captured her working to ring up purchases, a line of customers forming.

Gus shifted his attention to what was happening in the parking lot in front of the convenience store.

Ned Little Foot carried a large trash bag and appeared to be collecting garbage littering the premises. He picked up an empty plastic bottle, stuffed it into the bag and moved on, passing another bottle without bending to collect it. He paused to nod and greet a customer and kept moving toward the end of the parking area.

"The cash register was acting up here," Peyton pointed to the video depicting what was happening inside the store. "I remember everyone was getting sassy and impatient. Ned had disappeared, so I had to figure it out without him." She shook her head. "It's all surreal like this happened in another life."

When Gus turned back to the video footage from the camera on the front of the building, Ned had reached the two vehicles parked the furthest out.

"My car was the one on the left." Peyton used the mouse and the cursor to point at the vehicle beside hers. "The Mustang convertible is Ned's. He purchased it the day before and was so proud of it. He said it was the first new car he'd ever owned. Like me, he couldn't afford new and usually purchased used cars."

Ned circled the bright red Mustang, running his hand across the paint.

He glanced toward the store entrance and then ducked between his car and Peyton's.

"Did he fall?" Peyton asked.

Gus shook his head. "I don't think so. Go back a few seconds."

Peyton backed the video up to the point Ned had ducked and froze the frame.

Gus pointed to the monitor. "Can you enlarge his hand?"

Peyton moved the mouse and clicked, zooming in on Ned's hand. Her heart sank into her gut and churned, making her want to vomit. "That goddamn bastard set me up."

Pure rage boiled up inside Gus.

Though grainy, it was obvious. Ned held a screwdriver in his hand.

Peyton leaped from the chair and ran out into the hallway.

Gus quickly shut down the computer and followed Peyton out of the office. "We need to have words with your old boss."

Peyton stood in front of an annual calendar affixed to the wall. "He planned this with them all along," she said, her voice low, strained. "Look." She pointed to the date she'd disappeared. "I remember looking at this calendar as I was leaving that night. He had other employees scheduled over the month. I asked why he hadn't posted my schedule. He said he must've made a mistake and for me to check with him the next day."

Gus studied the calendar with names and times written all over it from the beginning of the year through the next month.

"Ned always planned the schedule a month out.

When it changed, he crossed through the name and wrote the new one." She looked up into Gus's eyes. "He never intended to put me on the schedule. He knew I wouldn't be available. The bastard sold me into that hell. That would also explain how he came up with enough money to buy a brand-new sports car. This store doesn't generate that much of a profit." She spun, heading for the door.

Gus followed. "Where are you going?"

"To find Ned and beat the hell out of him." As she reached for the handle of the rear exit door, Gus laid a hand over hers.

"You can't do that," he said.

"The hell I can't."

"Not yet." Gus squeezed her hand. "He's only a link in the chain of people responsible. And, like you said, you can't be seen until we free the others."

Peyton stood still, her cheeks flaming, breathing hard, her chest rising and falling as if she'd been running. "He sold me out."

"And he'll pay for it," Gus reassured her. "*After* we find and free the others."

"Then let's do it. These people can't continue to get away with what they're doing." Tears welled in her eyes. "They've destroyed so many lives."

"Come on, let's get out of here." Gus twisted the doorknob and tugged it toward him.

"Wait!" Peyton slammed it shut before he'd gotten it even halfway open.

"What?" he asked, surprised by her sudden move.

"Headlights." Peyton pressed her ear against the door; a moment later, she jerked back. "Shit. Shit. Shit. A car door just slammed. Hurry. Hide."

She started for the office, changed direction and ducked into a supply closet with barely enough room for the big mop bucket on wheels and the array of brooms and mops. Scooting back as far as she could go, she snagged the front of Gus's shirt and dragged him in as the back door swung open. The man Peyton had identified in the video as Ned Little Foot stepped inside, struggling to pull the key from the lock.

Gus turned and pulled the closet door toward him, leaving a narrow gap, small enough Ned wouldn't see inside but big enough Gus could see out and follow the man's movements.

Peyton eased around to Gus's side and beneath his arm to peer through the crack.

Ned gave up on the key in the lock, left it and rushed for the office. Desk drawers slammed open and closed, and cabinet doors opened and slammed.

"He seems agitated, in a hurry," Peyton whispered.

The thunk of something heavy hitting a wall was soon followed by the sound of a metal door closing.

"He's getting into his safe," Peyton said. "Do you think he knows where they're keeping the trailers?"

"I don't know," Gus said, an idea forming. "Look, you can't be seen, but they don't know me. We need to question your boss. If he knows where they are, we're that much closer to getting them out of that situation. But I won't step out of this closet unless you swear on those women's lives that you'll stay put no matter what."

She held up a hand. "I swear I'll stay put."

Gus prepared to step out of the closet, hoping to do that before Ned came out into the hallway.

He had his hand on the door, about to push it open, when Ned emerged from his office with a satchel over his shoulder and carrying a box.

He'd only taken a step toward the back door when two large men pushed through.

Peyton smothered a gasp and shrank back against Gus.

"What are you doing here?" Ned demanded. "None of you were ever supposed to show your faces around the store. It's too dangerous."

The man in the lead looked like he could be a bouncer at a biker bar with his broad shoulders, thick arms and meaty fists. He sported a shaggy beard and a mustache that hung down over his lips. "Snake sent us."

Gus suspected as much when Peyton had backed into him, her body trembling. She recognized these men. Gus's first inclination was to jump out of the closet and smash his fist into each one of these men's faces. It took every bit of his control to resist. There were three of them and one of him. If he left the closet, they might see Peyton. Even if they didn't, he might not win a fight with the odds stacked three to one. When they beat him to a pulp, he wouldn't be able to protect Peyton.

So, he remained hidden in the closet. They could not know she was there.

Ned shifted the strap holding the satchel on his shoulder. "Good. You tell Snake I'm not happy about this situation. He promised they'd never leave his control. And now, one's missing?" He shook his head, the motion jerky. "I'm not happy. What if she goes to the authorities? What if she brings them here? What's he doing to clean up this mess?"

The second man stepped up beside the first. Not quite as massive as the first guy, he was tall, wiry and with tattoos across the tops of his hands, disappearing into the sleeve of his jacket. "He sent us to tie up loose ends."

Ned nodded. "So, is she headed here? Are you going to make sure she doesn't talk? I should've known she would be the one to get away. She was going to college, that one. Did you know that? She's smart. Probably too smart. Well, she's not here yet. But you're welcome to stay and wait for her. I'm getting out of town until this dies down. I don't like it when there are too many loose ends."

"Neither does Snake," the bouncer dude said.

Ned hesitated and then marched forward. "I get that. Now, if you'll excuse me, I'll be on my way."

When he came abreast of the two men, they parted enough to let him come between them.

Before Ned could pass them and head for the door, the wiry guy's arm hooked around and slammed into Ned.

Gus couldn't see what that arm had done, but it hadn't been good for Ned.

The convenience store owner stiffened. His hands rose to his front. "What the—"

The big guy with the beard leaned close to Ned's ear, "Snake doesn't like loose ends." Then he bumped the man with his shoulder.

Ned staggered backward, falling on his ass. At this point, Gus could see that his hands were clasped around the hilt of a knife. He looked down at the blood soaking his gray T-shirt, swayed and fell onto his back, his head coming to rest in front of the crack in the supply closet door.

Gus tensed.

If the two men bent to check if Ned was truly dead, they might see into the closet. Gus had to be prepared to defend himself, but mostly, he had to defend Peyton, their other loose end he was certain Snake would eliminate just like Ned.

The slimmer guy bent to retrieve the knife jutting from Ned's chest.

"Is he dead?" Bouncer Guy asked.

"Damn right, he is," Knife Dude responded, wiping the blade off on Ned's shirt.

"If he ain't, he will be soon." Bouncer Guy lifted his chin. "Let's get it done and get out of here."

"I'll be glad after tomorrow night. We won't have to deal with those women anymore."

"That's a dumb thing to say. We have jobs because of them," Bouncer said. "I don't know why he thinks he has to get rid of them. The best bet is to keep moving. We could find a place to lay low for a while until we know for sure what happened to that bitch. Then we can set up shop away from here." He pulled open the back door and stepped outside.

"That makes more sense than getting rid of the merchandise." The door swung closed behind the two men.

Gus stayed put for several more seconds, his gaze fixed on the exit.

"Do you think they'll come back?" Peyton asked, her body trembling against his.

He wrapped an arm around her and pulled her closer. "No, but let's stay here a few minutes in case they do."

Gus held her until she quit trembling, his senses on alert for the bad guys, but also tuned into how Peyton felt pressed against him. The scent of her shampoo directly beneath his nose and the way her body pressed into his was doing crazy things to him.

"Are you okay?" he whispered, ready to drop his arm away from her should she spook and want to be free.

"I'm okay." She raised her hand to drape across his, where it rested over her belly. "Better than okay when I'm with you. Thank you." She turned in his arms, rose on her toes and brushed her lips across his. "Thank you."

His arm clasped her around the waist and dragged her closer. He moved slowly and gently. With the smallest amount of pressure, he allowed her the choice to stay or go.

Gus tipped her chin up and stared into her eyes in the little light shining in through the crack in the door. "I want to kiss you," he whispered.

Her eyes widened. "You do?"

He nodded. *"Really* kiss you." He pressed his forehead against hers. "But I don't want to scare you."

"I'm not scared of you kissing me," she said. "I'm more afraid you won't."

The invitation in her words and her expression were almost his undoing. Gus had to remind himself that a dead man was lying on the floor outside the door. That fact alone should be enough to kill his libido. Add the more immediate danger of the two men lurking outside the building, who would kill them without hesitation if they discovered them hiding in the closet, and he'd be a fool to start something he couldn't finish or do justice to.

He drew a deep breath and let it out slowly, then pulled her close, tipped her head downward and pressed his lips to her forehead. "Hold that thought.

As much as I want to kiss you, I need to get you somewhere safe before I lose my mind."

When her lips turned downward and she looked away, he couldn't take it. He captured her chin. "It's not a matter of *if* I'll kiss you," he said. "It's *when*." He brushed his thumb across her bottom lip. "It will happen—when I have time to do it right. Now, I need you to stay hidden in here while I see if those men are gone."

"I'll stay." Peyton backed away as far as she could get in the small space.

Gus slipped through the door, closing it to only a sliver of an opening. He quickly checked Ned for a pulse, not wanting to be surprised by a miraculous rising from the dead.

No pulse.

He stepped over the dead man and crossed to the door.

When he wrapped his hand around the doorknob, it felt warm. Then he smelled the smoke.

"Is that smoke I smell?" Peyton poked her head out the door of the closet.

"It is," Gus reached for her hand. "That door's hot. Where's another door?"

"This way," she said, leading him down the hall-way, through the stock room and into the store.

Light shone through the windows, not from the streetlights or interior lights. Flames billowed up in front of the store, staining the interior red and orange.

Beyond the wall of flames, a white van spun out of the parking lot.

But that wasn't what caught Gus's attention, sending fear all the way to his bones. The flames rose around them and spread outward toward the fuel pumps.

He grabbed Peyton's hand and spun in the opposite direction. "Run!"

CHAPTER 14

PEYTON RACED through the store behind Gus. Smoke from outside seeped through cracks as the fire ignited the exterior walls.

By the time they reached the back door, they had to crouch to stay below the cloud of smoke.

"Stand back," Gus yelled, dragging her to stand behind him. He ripped off his jacket, wrapped it around the doorknob, yanked the door open and stepped away from the door.

Heat and flames roared in—a wall of destruction between them and fresh, clean air.

"Those pumps could blow any moment," Peyton said, her skin heating.

Gus nodded. "We have to make a run for it."

"I'm ready," she said.

"Not yet." He draped his jacket over her head.

"Hold onto this, close your eyes and run. I'll make sure you get to the other side."

"No," she said. "You need your jacket." When she tried to give it back to him, he headed for the door. "It's time."

She pulled the jacket over her head and held it together with one hand, placing her other hand in his.

"Breath in and...*go!*" Gus yelled and burst through the door, taking Peyton with him.

Holding her breath, she followed Gus through the flames. When the heat and smoke were too much, she closed her eyes and trusted him to get her to the other side.

One moment, she was engulfed in smoke and flame. The next, she was on the other side, breathing in fresh night air.

Her natural inclination was to slow down and take deep breaths of smoke-free air, but Gus kept going, taking her with him.

Boom!

The explosion rocked the ground beneath them.

Peyton stumbled and fell to her knees.

Gus covered her with his body.

Sirens sounded in the distance, heading their way.

"Are you okay?" Gus pushed to his feet and bent to help her up.

"I am," she said, surprised that the explosion hadn't been as bad as she'd expected,

They looked back at the burning building. Flames burned bright and hot, reaching up into the night sky.

"Thankfully, the store shielded us from the gas pump explosion." Gus cupped her elbow. "We need to be gone before the police and firefighters arrive. They might think we killed Ned and started the fire."

Gus set the pace at a quick walk, ducking into whatever shadows they found along the way back to the rusted shipping container, behind which they'd parked his truck.

"Where to?" Peyton asked.

"West Yellowstone," Gus said.

She glanced over her shoulder as they left Riverton behind. As the fire and the city's lights faded in the distance, she turned to face the road ahead.

"I grew up on this reservation. It was my home all my life." She stared out at the plains bathed in starlight. "Now, I don't feel like I belong here. Or anywhere else, for that matter."

Gus reached across the console for her hand.

She took it and held on to his strength.

"I'm not sure I felt like I belonged, even before I was taken. The only family I have left here, my aunt and uncle, didn't want anything to do with me. I don't know why I stayed. And now, I find out that even my boss didn't give two shits about me. He sold me for a Mustang." She laughed, the sound strangled by the sob lodged in her throat.

"I'm sorry," Gus said.

"Don't feel sorry for me." Peyton squared her shoulders and lifted her chin. "This was a huge wake-up call. If I want something different, I have to stop doing the same thing while expecting different results. And I want to help people who, through no fault of their own, have experienced life-altering trauma. Like Hannah."

"You'd be good at it," Gus said.

"And I will get there. I didn't survive what I did just to crawl back under a rock."

Gus pulled his cell phone out of his pocket and glanced down at it. "No signal. I need to remember to call Stone and Hank and let them know what happened."

"I wish we could've followed those two men," Peyton said. "They're probably heading back to the trailers as we speak."

"We'll find them," Gus assured her. "You heard Snake's hit men. They're holding one more event."

"We have to find them before that event is over. We can't let Snake move on to find a place to dispose of however many women he has locked up in those trailers."

. . .

ALMOST TWO HOURS LATER, Peyton blinked her eyes open and stared out at the scenery around them. Behind them, the sun was peeking over the edge of the horizon. A town spread out before them. As they entered, a sign proclaimed the town to be West Yellowstone.

Gus drove through the town and almost out again before turning off the main road. He brought the truck to a stop in a parking lot and shifted into park.

A rustic lodge spread out in front of them.

"Welcome to the Grand Yellowstone Lodge," Gus said. "We'll stay here until we hear something from Hank and Swede—which I expect to happen soon."

Peyton stretched. "Until we hear something from him, I'd like to take the time to shower and maybe get a couple of hours of sleep."

"I can help make that happen." With a tired grin, he pushed open the truck door and dropped to the ground.

He rounded the hood in time to assist Peyton from her seat to the ground.

She swayed slightly.

Immediately, Gus's arm came around her. "Come on, let's get you to a shower and a bed. You look like you wrestled a bonfire and didn't exactly win."

She grimaced. "That sounds attractive."

"What's attractive is the smudge of soot on your nose." He winked and pulled a key card from his wallet. "Let's hope this still works. Stone Jacobs, my boss, assured me that my room is as I left it over a month ago. Hopefully, this key card will get us into the room. It's still early. I'm not sure anyone mans the registration counter before seven. We can get you a room of your own once they're open. In the meantime, you're welcome to use my room and shower."

"I'd love a shower. And I'd be willing to sleep on the floor if it means I can get a couple of hours of rest."

Gus shook his head. "You can have the bed. I'll take the floor."

Peyton opened her mouth, thought better, then closed it. "I'd argue, but I'm too tired. You must be exhausted. At least I got to sleep during some of the time it took to get here."

Gus slung his bag over his shoulder, handed one of Peyton's bundles to her and took the other. Then he offered her his free arm.

She slid her hand through the crook of his elbow. Peyton was getting used to leaning on him. Unfortunately, that wouldn't last forever. They'd free the women, put Snake and his cohorts behind bars and Gus would be assigned another mission.

What would she do when he moved on to his next mission?

She'd learn to get on with her life. Alone.

Gus used his key card to open the exterior door and held it while Peyton passed through. He led her across the lobby with the two-story cathedral ceiling and up a set of stairs to the second floor. He continued down a long hallway, stopping halfway in front of a door where he ran his card over the lock. A lock clicked, a little light blinked green and he pushed the door open and waited for Peyton to enter before he followed.

The room was spacious, with a king-sized bed, a dresser, a desk and a loveseat in one corner near a set of French doors. The adjoining bathroom had a long granite countertop, dual sinks and a shower big enough for two people.

"This is nice," Peyton said.

"You can have the first shower. I'm going down to the kitchen to raid the refrigerator for something to eat. If we want to sleep in, we'll miss breakfast. Unless you only want an hour-long nap so that you can join the team for a big, noisy breakfast."

Peyton shook her head. "I'd love a snack and a longer sleep."

"I'm also going to brief my boss on what happened in Riverton. He needs to let everyone know that Snake plans on this being the last event for the current captives. Hopefully, that won't take too long. I'll be back about the time you're finished in the shower."

When Gus left her alone in the room, Peyton untied her bundle of clothing and found the silky nightgown, panties and her toiletries.

Armed with her things, she entered the bathroom,

turned on the shower and stripped out of the smoky clothing.

Peyton made quick work of scrubbing the soot from her hair and every inch of her body. Once she was done, she rinsed and stood for a long soak beneath the spray before shutting off the water and reaching for a towel. If Gus hadn't needed a shower after her, she would have stood longer beneath the spray, hoping that, eventually, she'd feel as clean inside as she was on the outside. Maybe with time.

She dressed in the silky nightgown, brushed the tangles from her hair and let it fall down her back, straight and thick.

When she emerged from the bathroom, she expected to find Gus back from the kitchen. Her tummy rumbled at the thought of food.

Footsteps sounded in the hallway,

Peyton pressed her eye to the peephole and stared through its distorted lens into the hallway.

Gus stood in front of the door, holding a large tray filled with a variety of snacks, from an array of various kinds of cheeses to a plate full of scrambled eggs and bacon.

Peyton snatched open the door and stepped back, only then realizing she was dressed in the silky gown that did little to hide her figure.

Gus didn't stare or comment on her attire as if he found it natural for her to pad around his room so scantily clad.

She was a little disappointed that he didn't say whether or not he liked the gown, but she really was too tired to care.

Gus entered, carrying the tray past her to the desk against the wall. "Cookie was already up, scrambling eggs, frying bacon and sausages and making toast. Between the two of us, we have enough food to feed a village."

"Wow," Peyton said. "That looks and smells amazing."

He set the tray on the desk. "Grab a plate and a fork, and dig in. And it's your choice of beverage. I brought some of each. Orange juice, milk and coffee."

Peyton stared at all the food, eager, excited and all of a sudden...sad. Tears welled in her eyes. "They didn't feed us much. Half a bologna sandwich and a cup of water was a treat. Sometimes, they'd give us peanut butter and crackers. I'd dream about scrambled eggs and bacon." A tear slipped down her cheek. She wiped it away.

"It's hard to eat so well knowing those other women aren't," he stated.

She nodded. Another tear slid down her cheek. "I'm sorry."

"Don't be sorry." He took her hands in his. "You have to think of eating as fueling your body for what comes next. You need strength to help free them. And once they're free, you'll want to help them adjust. You'll need every bit of your emotional and physical strength. So, eat. For them."

Peyton looked at the tray again, remembering how weak she'd been when she'd escaped. She'd only just begun to regain her strength.

"Okay. I'll eat to keep up my physical strength. Then I'll rest to restore my emotional and mental health."

She loaded her plate with food that would fuel her body and ate, knowing it was only a matter of time until they found the trailers and rescued the women.

When she had consumed the plate of food, her eyelids drooped. She could barely keep them open.

"Go ahead," Gus tipped his head toward the bed. "Sleep in the bed. I still have to get a shower. Then I'll camp out on the floor. And don't worry. I've slept on worse."

Peyton didn't bother telling him that she'd slept on worse. It wasn't something she wanted to share with anyone.

She ducked into the bathroom to relieve herself and brush her teeth. As she came out, Gus went in carrying his shaving kit.

He still smelled of smoke and had soot smeared across his face.

Even with the layer of filth, he was a handsome man any woman would easily fall in love with. Peyton was no exception. After so many men had treated her so badly, she'd been certain there weren't any good men left.

Until Gus. A man who opened doors for a woman. Who helped in any way that he could to make her life easier. He was well on his way to restoring her faith in men. Well, in one man.

Peyton climbed into the bed, pulled the blanket up to her chin and reveled in the clean scents and softness against her skin. She closed her eyes, meaning to stay awake until Gus came out of the bathroom, at which time she intended to move to the floor so that he could sleep in the bed. She didn't last two minutes before she was asleep.

Almost as soon as she drifted off, the dreams commenced.

She was back in the trailer, naked, cold and hungry. Men were queuing at the door, paying their money and demanding their turn.

Peyton dragged herself to her feet, desperate to leave, determined to get out before it all happened again. There were no doors in this room, just a window covered in black trash bags and duct tape. If she could tear away the tape and plastic, maybe she could climb out the window and run and hide in the woods. She didn't have clothes or shoes, but it didn't matter. She'd rather die in the woods than die in the trailer.

A woman moaned in another room.

If she escaped, she'd be leaving the other captives behind.

But only until she could get help. Then she'd be back.

Digging her fingers beneath the line of tape, she pulled it back, tearing the black trash bags off the window. Light pushed through the dirty glass, dispelling the gloom. With the window exposed, Peyton searched for the latch and slid the window sideways.

Smoke filled the room.

Peyton dove through the window but got stuck halfway there. Footsteps pounded into the room behind her. Someone grabbed her ankles and pulled her back inside.

She clung to the window with all her might, praying whoever had her would let go. She wanted to scream for help but was afraid the line of men waiting to come into the trailer would find her, and it would be all over before she even touched her feet to the ground.

She fought to free her feet, to escape the trailer. Hands gripped her arms.

"No," she murmured. "Please don't."

"Peyton," a deep, warm voice sounded in her ear.

"No," she said.

"Peyton, wake up," the voice said.

"Escape," she said. "Help me."

"Sweetheart," the voice said. "Everything's okay. You're safe." Arms circled her. Instead of confining her and holding her back, they wrapped around her like a shield.

She could withstand any assault as long as she had her shield.

"You're safe."

She eventually relaxed, cocooned in arms there to hold and protect, not trap and imprison.

Peyton nestled against warm skin, her terror fading as she surfaced from the nightmare. When she opened her eyes, her immediate view was of a man's naked chest, a chin with a five-o'clock shadow and a gentle smile.

"Hey." Gus's voice wrapped around her, resonating against her ear from deep in his chest. "Are you awake now?"

She nodded, heat rising up her neck into her face when she realized her hand rested on his chest...skin-to-skin.

"I'm sorry," she said, drawing the hand away.

He gathered her fingers and raised them to his lips. "Don't be sorry."

"You shouldn't have to babysit me. I should be stronger."

"You've been through so much. I still have night-mares," he admitted. "And I don't consider this babysitting. I consider it a good excuse to hold you in my arms." He tipped her chin up. "But if it makes you uncomfortable, I'll move away. With me, you have the choice. I will never do anything you don't want me to do."

He held her gaze for a long moment.

"Do you want me to go?"

"No," she responded without hesitation, her hand curling around his. "Please. Stay."

His arm tightened around her, bringing her body closer to his.

She melted into him, loving how solid he felt against her. "What about your choice?" she whispered. "You don't have to do this."

"Sweetheart, I've wanted to hold you since the moment I realized you weren't Franklin beneath that horse blanket."

"How could you want to hold me then?" She shook her head slowly, remembering how cold and alone she'd been. "I was dirty and probably smelled."

"You were like a stray kitten, desperately hungry but fierce and determined to be free. I wanted to hold you and let you know you were safe."

"So, I'm a stray kitten you want to rescue from the cold?" she asked.

"Maybe at first," Gus admitted. "But you're so much more." He brushed a strand of her hair back from her cheek and pressed a kiss to her forehead. "You aren't as worried about your own safety as the safety of others. You could've walked away and forgotten them, but you won't."

"Can't," she whispered.

He nodded. "Can't. Even when you were weak, you were strong in your determination to get back to them."

"No one was coming to our rescue," she said. "If I don't go after them, who will?"

He tipped her chin up. "Thus, the reason I've

wanted to hold you. You're a good human. Beautiful inside and out."

Peyton stared up at him, her heart swelling in her chest, bolstering her courage to ask for what she wanted. "Is now the time?"

His brow twisted, and his lips twitched into a smile. "The time for what?"

Encouraged by his gentle, teasing smile, she met his gaze and held it. "That kiss."

His lips spread into a grin that immediately pinched into a frown. "I don't know. It might be too soon. You need time to recover from...everything. I don't want to frighten you or take advantage of a weak moment."

"Do you want to kiss me?" she asked.

He gave a sharp bark of laughter. "Yes!"

"And didn't you just tell me I have a choice?"

He nodded.

Peyton leaned up on her elbow. "I choose that kiss. Now."

He cupped the back of her head and drew her close until her lips were a breath away from his.

"You have to want this. I would never force you to do something that makes you uncomfortable."

"*Not* kissing you is making me uncomfortable," she said and pressed her lips to his.

His fingers threaded through the hair at the back of her neck, applying a little pressure as he deepened the kiss.

He opened to her, his tongue seeking, curling around hers in a primal dance that left her breathless and wanting so much more than a kiss.

She raised her head, her lips leaving his long enough to inhale. Peyton stared down at his beautiful, rugged face. "You make me want you."

His lips spread into a smile. "Is that a bad thing?"

Her brow twisted. "I don't know. I swore that if I ever got away from that situation, I'd never let another man touch me. I'd never *want* a man to touch me."

Gus's brow dipped. "Oh, sweetheart, I don't blame you. And if a kiss is all you want from me, I'm okay with that."

She shook her head. "I was so sure..." Her mind churned through her confusion. "Now...I'm not."

He captured her cheeks between his hands and brushed a light kiss across her lips. "It's too soon. You're not ready. And that's okay."

"You don't understand," she whispered. "I *want* you. I want more than a kiss." She caught her lower lip between her teeth. "But I'm afraid."

"It's okay to be afraid." Gus brushed his thumb across her lip, freeing it from her teeth. "You were raped. Forced to do things you had no control over. You need time to heal." He scooted over. "Lay down. Rest. You're free now."

She settled against him, her body still humming, her core hot, desire raging through her alongside confusion. Peyton wanted to be naked with this man, wanted to feel his hands on her body. Wanted him moving inside her.

Was it too soon?

Probably.

She barely knew Gus. But he was kind, gentle and protective.

Was she attracted to him because he was the first man to be nice to her?

Maybe?

No.

Not entirely.

The man was attractive, undemanding and incredibly patient.

Was she scared?

Hell, yes.

"I know what it feels like to be raped," she said softly.

His arm tightened around her.

Her throat tightened on a wad of emotion. "I want to know what it feels like to make love."

"And you will," he murmured. "Make sure it's when you're ready, not when you think it's what your partner wants." He snorted. "If I happen to be that partner, I can tell you, it's what I want. You're beautiful, brave and incredibly desirable."

"Even after being used?" she whispered.

"Peyton." He rose on his elbow and stared down into her eyes. "Don't think any less of yourself because of what they did to you." He held her gaze for a moment. "I don't."

Tears slipped from the corners of her eyes, "I can't help it," she said, her words choking on a sob. "I still feel...dirty. Like no decent man could possibly love me or want to...make love to me...after what happened."

"Honey," he said. "I want to make love to you so much right now that I'll be hurting for a while. But I won't. Not because I think you're dirty, but because I'm not those other men. It's not all about me. Making love should be a mutual experience. You should feel safe and cherished throughout. And your needs and desires should be satisfied, not ignored."

The passion in Gus's voice resonated inside Peyton.

He pressed a kiss to her forehead and one to the tip of her nose. "Don't settle for less." He lay beside her, gathered her into his arms and closed his eyes. "Now, get some rest. I have a feeling the shit's gonna get real, and soon. We need to be ready."

Peyton curled into Gus's side, warm, protected and turned on.

He was right to wait.

She had issues she needed to work through before she made love to a man.

Peyton hoped Gus would still want her when she found herself on the other side.

CHAPTER 15

Loud knocking jerked Gus from a deep sleep.

Peyton sat up beside him, pushing the hair out of her face. "What's going on?"

"I don't know."

The knocking resumed. "Gus! Wake up!" a man's voice called out.

Gus leaped out of the bed and hurried to open the door.

Stone Jacobs stood on the other side, a frown creasing his forehead. "Get dressed and meet us in the war room." He looked past Gus to Peyton. "Bring Peyton. Make it quick. This is time-sensitive. We have to move on it quickly."

"Roger. We'll be right there." Gus closed the door and strode toward his duffel bag, shooting a glance toward Peyton. "You heard that?"

"I heard." Already out of bed, awake and alert, she

darted into the bathroom.

Gus pulled on a clean pair of jeans, a T-shirt and his boots.

A minute later, Peyton emerged, hair brushed back and secured in a ponytail, her face freshly washed. She dug through the bundles of clothes Sadie McClain had given her and pulled out jeans, a long-sleeved sweater and a jean jacket.

Gus took his turn in the bathroom, relieved himself, combed his hair and brushed his teeth. By the time he came out, Peyton was dressed and pulling on a pair of boots.

Gus slung his leather jacket over his shoulder. "Ready?"

She nodded.

He held the door open for her.

Once they were both in the hallway, she slipped her hand into his.

"Where's the war room?" she asked.

"I'll show you." Gus led her through the lodge and out the back door. They crossed the yard and hurried down the path to the barn.

She looked up at what appeared to be just a big old barn from the outside. "It's in there?"

He grinned and led her around to stairs on the side that led up into what had once been the loft.

At the top of the stairs, he pressed his thumb to a bio scanner, a lock clicked, and he opened the door.

Inside was a different world. Bright white walls, a

long, sleek conference table with a screen at the far end, a technical center with keyboards and an array of monitors.

The entire Yellowstone contingent of the Brotherhood Protectors was seated at the table. Kyla Russell, Stone's fiancée, was among them, a laptop opened in front of her.

When Peyton stepped through the door, the men rose as one.

Stone stepped forward and held out his hand to Peyton. "Ms. Running Bear, I'm Stone Jacobs. It's a pleasure to meet you."

She gave him a tentative smile. "Thank you for helping me."

"We haven't done much yet," Stone said. "But we think that's about to change."

Gus stood close to her side, worried that having all these men crowded into the room would overwhelm Peyton.

Stone held out his hand to Gus. "Welcome back, Gus. Nothing like jumping in with both feet on your first day back, eh?"

Gus nodded. "It's good to be back."

Stone waved toward the men in the room. "Ms. Running Bear, these are the men of the Brotherhood Protectors, Yellowstone division. As he pointed to each man, he introduced them. "Ben Yates, Navy SEAL. Carter Manning, Navy SEAL. Dax Young, Navy SEAL. Moe Cleveland, Air Force PJ. Hunter

Falcon, Delta Force. Cliff Cranston, Navy SEAL. Our tech support for this district is Kyla Russell, retired assassin and my fiancée." He turned back to Gus. "And you know Gus Walsh, Navy SEAL. Please, take a seat."

Gus escorted Peyton to the table and held her chair while she took her seat.

Stone nodded to Kyla. "Kujo, one of Hank's operatives, received word this morning that the caravan of trailers shows up at major events where there's a predominantly male population. The last one was the Livingston Rodeo." He nodded toward Peyton. "That's why you ended up at the truck stop in Livingston. Kyla and Swede crosschecked against the schedule of events in the region. The next major gathering is here at the West Yellowstone Rodeo. It started last night and ends tonight. We think this man Peyton identified as Snake will have people in the crowd, spreading the word to cowboys looking to blow off some steam." Stone glanced around the table. "We need to be one or some of those cowboys they invite. Gus, I've already briefed everyone else. We'll equip the team with earbud communications devices and tracking discs."

"It's important to remember that Snake plans on this being the last event for this group of captives," Gus said. "We have one shot. We can't miss."

Stone nodded. "That's why the entire team will be spread out among the rodeo participants and spectators. We'll have a better chance of getting an invite. Hank's also staging a helicopter at the West Yellowstone regional airport. We can have it up, searching for the trailers during the rodeo."

"Wait. No." Peyton held up a hand. "If you have a helicopter hovering over the trailers, Snake might get spooked and close up shop before we can get in to rescue those women."

Stone's eyes narrowed. "Good point. We'll keep them on standby in case we need to drop some of our guys close and have them move in on foot."

"When do we plan on being at the rodeo?" Peyton asked.

"As soon as we gear up," Stone said. "You're all supposed to be there as cowboys, part of the rodeo circuit. You'll need to dress the part."

"I'll need a disguise," Peyton said. "If I dress as a boy, Snake's men will be less likely to recognize me."

Gus frowned. He hadn't even considered including Peyton in this operation. "You're not going. It's too dangerous."

Peyton's lips pressed together, and a dent formed at the bridge of her nose. "I'm the only one who can recognize all the men who work for Snake. If this is our only shot at locating the trailers, you need me there. I can identify the men you need to target to secure the invite and location. You need me there."

Gus wanted to argue the point, but Peyton was right. They couldn't leave it to chance.

"You only go if you stay with me," Gus said.

Her lips softened. "Believe me, I'll be at your side. I have no intention of being caught by Snake and his men."

"The rodeo events go until nine o'clock, followed by a concert," Stone said. "We need to be in place no later than midafternoon, mingling and hanging out with contestants. Let's get geared up."

While Kyla distributed earbud radios to each man and Peyton, Stone opened the armory and handed out weapons they'd need for an extraction mission. The rifles would remain in their respective vehicles. Most of the men, including Gus, had their own knives either clipped to their belts or strapped around their calves. Gus opted for a shoulder holster with a .9-millimeter pistol tucked in it and an AR-15 rifle he would store behind the seat of his pickup.

Peyton pulled Gus to the side. "Kyla is going to help me with my disguise. I'll meet you back in your room."

Gus frowned. "I can come with you," he said. "I'm finished here."

Peyton smiled. "I'll be fine with Kyla. I won't be long. I want to get to the rodeo sooner than the others so I can identify some of Snake's men by the time they filter in."

Gus's gut tightened. He and Peyton had been together practically since the moment he'd pounced on her from the haystack at Brighter Days. He wasn't ready to let her out of his sight.

Kyla joined them. "Don't worry. I'll take good care of her." Without giving Gus or Peyton a chance to think about it, she snagged Peyton's arm and led her out of the war room loft.

"Take some zip ties and duct tape." Stone was saying. "You never know when they'll come in handy. And don't underestimate the power of a stun gun. For those who need one, I have extra cowboy hats in my room. And Cookie has lunch ready."

Gus filled his pockets with zip ties, duct tape and two stun guns. He left the war room, descended the stairs and walked back to the lodge, his thoughts on Peyton. Kyla was the perfect choice to help with Peyton's disguise. The woman had been an assassin. She'd know best how to blend into any crowd.

The little devil on his shoulder reminded him *Kyla was an assassin.*

Not that she was anymore—and she'd proven herself as trustworthy and dedicated to the Brotherhood Protectors. After all, Hank had been instrumental in extracting her, along with the team of men who now made up the core of the Yellowstone division of the Brotherhood Protectors.

The bottom line was that Gus preferred to be the one protecting Peyton. He couldn't do that if she wasn't within sight.

He loaded the rifle in his truck and returned to

his room, changing into a more faded pair of jeans, then putting a button-down shirt over his T-shirt. The shoulder holster was next, and then he shrugged into his leather jacket. Finally, he reached into the closet for the cowboy hat he'd left there a month ago and fitted it on his head.

And still, Peyton hadn't returned.

Tired of waiting, he jerked open the door.

A boy stood in front of him, dressed in faded jeans, a long-sleeved chambray shirt, scuffed cowboy boots and a well-worn straw cowboy hat. "Sir, do you know where I can find Gus Walsh?"

He did a double-take. "Peyton?"

A grin spread across the boy's face. "Yeah, it's me."

Gus shook his head. "If I hadn't known you would be disguised as a boy, I wouldn't have guessed it was you." He pulled her through the door, closed it behind her, whipped off his hat and kissed her full on the lips.

She wrapped her arms around him and opened to him, meeting his tongue with hers.

When he came up for air, he nodded. "Yup, it's you."

She laughed. "Kyla did good." Her smile faded. "Are you ready?"

"Yeah, but first." He dug one of the stun guns out of his pocket, showed Peyton how to use it and tucked it into her back pocket. "Just in case."

She chuckled. "That's the kind of gift that says you care."

"Damn right it is." Then he retrieved his hat from where it had fallen on the floor. He didn't feel good about taking Peyton to the rodeo, where she might come in contact with the men who'd held her captive. He also knew that if he didn't take her, she'd go without him. It was better to take her and know where she was than for her to go off on her own. "I'm ready."

CHAPTER 16

AT THE RODEO, Gus and Peyton spent several hours sitting in the stands, walking through the carnival area and hanging out with some of the contestants as they waited for their events.

Peyton had yet to spot Snake or any of the men who worked for him. "Are we sure this is the event they would target next? There's not another one in the area going on at the same time?"

Stone's voice filled her ear, reminding her of the earbud she'd inserted hours ago. "They call it a rodeo circuit because the contestants go from event to event, hoping to win prize money. They don't tend to overlap dates, or contestants would have to choose, and the rodeos wouldn't have the major draws."

"Okay," she said. "Thanks for the clarification."

Gus grinned. "Not used to having other people in your head?"

Her lips twisted. "No."

They were walking through the area where horse and cattle trailers were parked side by side in a field. Men and women moved in and out of the parking lot, leading horses and carrying saddles and buckets of grain or water.

The more time that passed without any contact with Snake's men, the more anxious Peyton became. "What if we don't spot them? What if your guys don't get an invite? What's our plan B?"

"Swede is working on it," Stone spoke again into their earbuds. "They've been combing through satellite images of the area looking for the trailers. They started with a twenty-five-mile radius and will expand that radius as needed."

"Sounds like looking for a needle in a haystack."

They'd strolled through the trailer parking area twice already. "Let's go back to the arena," Peyton said. "They have to show up soon; it's getting dark."

Gus changed direction, cutting through a line of pickups. "You'd think they'd already be here, scoping out their potential customers before they make contact."

"*If* this rodeo is their target," Peyton said. "I'm not conv—" She ground to a halt. Something had caught her eye.

Gus continued a few steps before he turned. "What?"

Peyton backed up a few steps, coming to a standstill next to a white pickup with a broken taillight that had red duct tape plastered over the break.

Her pulse hammered through her veins, and her breathing grew ragged. Her gaze shot around, searching for familiar, evil faces. She didn't see any nearby, but she could feel their presence.

Gus walked back to her, shooting a look inside the cab of the pickup before he came to a stop beside her. "Breathe," he whispered.

Peyton wanted him to wrap his arms around her and tell her everything would be okay. He couldn't do that without blowing her cover as a young cowboy. Instead, she breathed in and out like he'd shown her before until her pulse slowed and her breathing returned to normal.

"They're here," Peyton said softly.

"Where?" Stone asked into the earbud.

"I don't know, but one of their trucks is in the parking area."

"Gus," Stone said. "You got that extract tracking device on you?"

"Tagging it now." Gus acted as if the wind had knocked his hat off. As he bent to retrieve it from the ground beside the pickup, he slapped the magnetic tracker against the chassis. When he straightened, he casually brushed dust from the brim of his hat. "Let's find them."

Peyton fell in step beside Gus, her gaze flitting right and left, and her heartbeat speeding and slowing in an erratic rhythm. They were there. This was happening.

A man wearing a gray sweatshirt and a baseball cap stood near one of the corrals where bulls were held for the bull riding event. When his head turned, Peyton's breath caught. "There," she said. Looking away from him, she spoke softly but clearly, "Tall man, gray sweatshirt, baseball cap by the bullpen. He's one of them."

"Ben, here," a voice said over the radio. "I have him in sight."

"Carter, here," another voice said. "I have your six."

The man in the baseball cap pushed away from the bullpen and disappeared into the stands. The voice coming over the loudspeaker finished announcing the winners of the previous event and reminded the audience of what was coming next. A wave of spectators poured out of the bleachers, heading for the concession stands and food trucks scattered in and around the arena.

Soon, Gus and Peyton were surrounded by men, women and children, all eager to grab a drink, a bite to eat or use the portable toilets.

Peyton looked around but couldn't see much. At five feet two, she was shorter than most of the adults around her.

In a rare gap between people, she thought she saw a familiar profile. When the man raised a hand to shade his eyes from the setting sun, Peyton gasped.

At that moment, he turned, and his gaze met hers.

Peyton stood rooted to the ground, panic rising like a tsunami inside her. He'd spotted her.

She tried to tell herself he couldn't possibly recognize her in the disguise Kyla had dressed her in. She'd almost convinced herself of that when Snake's scared lip curled up, emphasizing his evil snarl.

All of this happened within seconds. Just when she turned to let Gus know, someone screamed.

Then, a lot of people were screaming and running away from the bullpen, heading straight for where Gus and Peyton stood.

Peyton couldn't see what was happening.

"Holy shit," Gus said. "There's a bull loose. Run!" He grabbed Peyton's hand and dragged her through the crowd.

Ahead of them, a toddler stood, separated from his parents, terrified and screaming.

"Gus!" Peyton yelled. "Help him!"

Gus released his hold on Peyton and dove through the stampede. As he scooped the child up in his arms, the crowd closed around Peyton, blocking her view of Gus and his view of her.

Thick arms wrapped around her. She screamed and fought. In her struggle to be free, she lost her earbud.

With everyone around her screaming and

running and with a bull headed into the middle of the crowd, no one noticed she was screaming for an entirely different reason.

Then, she was shoved into the back of a food truck. Another one of Snake's men was there. He slapped duct tape over her mouth and secured her wrists behind her back with a zip tie.

Peyton kicked and writhed, fighting with every ounce of her strength.

The food truck lurched forward. The big man lost his grip and dropped her to the floor.

Peyton landed hard, the breath knocked out of her lungs.

The two men caught her legs and secured her ankles with another zip tie.

This couldn't be happening to her. She couldn't be captured. She'd rather die.

Then she remembered the tracker she'd slipped into her boot.

Hopefully, Snake's men wouldn't find it or take off her boots before Gus and the Brotherhood Protectors could get to her and the other women.

The food truck bumped and lurched across rough ground. The men standing over her held onto the food preparation counters until the truck reached the pavement, where the ride smoothed.

Minutes later, the vehicle came to a jerky stop. The two men who'd nabbed her flung open the back door of the truck and climbed out. One of them grabbed Peyton's ankles and yanked her to the edge of the floor.

The other man hooked his hands beneath her arms. Between the two of them, they carried her to a waiting pickup with only one working taillight. The tailgate had been lowered.

"Thought you could escape, did you?" Snake stood beside the truck, his lips pulled back in a sneer. "Too bad you didn't learn the first time. Now, you'll get to witness firsthand how I keep my promises." He jerked his head toward the truck bed.

The two men swung her up into the back.

She landed hard on the metal truck bed.

One of the men climbed up into the back of the truck with her. The other man climbed into the driver's side. Snake closed the tailgate and slid into the passenger seat. The truck pulled out onto the highway. Going where?

Peyton had no idea.

She prayed that either the tracking device in her boot or on the truck would lead Gus to her and the other women before Snake made good on his promise.

In the meantime, it wouldn't hurt for her to figure out how to free herself without alerting the man hovering over her. She'd done her best to hold a gap between her wrists when they'd cinched the tie. She hoped it was enough. They'd applied the zip ties around her ankles over her boots. All she had to do was slip her feet out of the boots…

As long as they didn't drug her, she might have a chance. She sure as hell wouldn't go down without a fight.

CHAPTER 17

As soon as Gus handed the toddler to his frantic mother, he heard the scream in his earbud.

He spun, expecting to find Peyton behind him, only to see a stampede of people rushing to get out of the path of the raging bull.

Rodeo clowns and men carrying electric cattle prods moved in quickly, turning the bull around and sending it back toward the bullpen where it belonged.

"Peyton!" Gus called out, straining to hear her response through the radio. He waded through the people to where he'd last seen her. "Peyton?"

"Gus? Peyton? Everyone all right?" Stone's voice came through loud and clear in Gus's earbud.

"I can't find Peyton," Gus said. "We were separated when the bull charged the crowd, and she's not responding on the radio."

"This is Ben," another voice sounded on the radio. "We lost our guy in the crush."

"Hey, guys, Moe here. I spoke with some of the rodeo crew who work the pens. They said someone tampered with the gates and let that bull loose on the crowd."

"Get the feeling this guy Snake knew we were here and staged a diversion?" Ben suggested.

"Guys, Stone here. I have all the tracking discs up on my device. All but two are in the vicinity of the rodeo. The one assigned to Peyton and the spare assigned to Gus."

"I tagged the truck Peyton identified as one they used to haul trailers," Gus said. "It had the broken taillight."

"Peyton's tracker is closing in on the one you tagged the truck with," Stone said. "Now, they're together at the same location, heading east."

"Snake told Peyton that if she escaped again, he'd kill all the other women," Gus said. "We have to get to them before that happens."

"Ben, Carter and Moe, meet me at the SUV. We'll do our best to catch them by road," Stone said. "Gus, Hunter, Dax and Cliff, get to the airport. If we can't catch them before they get to the trailers, the helicopter might have a better chance of getting you there first. Kyla is on alert. She'll guide the chopper to where they're taking Peyton."

Gus was already halfway to his truck. He didn't

wait for the other men who would join him. Finding each other in the sea of parked vehicles would take too long.

Once in his truck, Gus blew out of the parking area and burst onto the highway, turning north to the airport. Headlights behind him reassured him the others were close.

It was dark as he rolled into the airport.

Someone with a flashlight waved him to an open gate. He didn't slow until he spotted the helicopter, blades spinning on the tarmac.

Gus drove as close to the aircraft as he dared, slammed on his brakes, threw the truck into park and leaped out. He grabbed the AR-15 from behind the back seat and jammed loaded magazines into his jacket pockets.

Ducking low, he ran for the chopper and leaped through the door. Hunter, Dax and Cliff were right behind him. As soon as all four men boarded, the helicopter lifted off the ground and headed east.

The men on board handed the newcomers thick gloves and headsets. The one closest to Gus thumped his own chest. "I'm Tony." He waved to the other guy. "That's TJ."

The pilot's voice came through the headset, "Just got word from Hank and Swede. Based on the direction the tracking devices were headed, they shifted their review of satellite images and found what looks like the trailers parked on an old logging road in the hills. We can get you to the other side of the ridge from the trailer location five minutes before the vehicle arrives with Ms. Running Bear. You'll have to fast-rope to the ground. The guys trailing them on the ground will get there a few minutes afterward. Five minutes isn't much time to get over the ridge and down to the trailers."

"It's five minutes more than if we were following behind them in vehicles," Gus said. "We'll take it."

"Get ready, then," the pilot said, "because we're here."

Thick ropes were lowered from both sides of the helicopter.

Gus slung the rifle over his shoulder and was first out. He slid down the rope to the ground, followed quickly by the other members of his team, as well as TJ and Tony. He didn't wait for all of the men to touch down before he slipped over the ridge and began his descent toward the bottom of the hill, where he could see the outlines of the trailers reflected in the starlight. As he neared the site, he slowed and picked his way closer, locating the men positioned as guards.

"We have two men on each trailer," Gus reported, speaking softly into his radio.

"There are two on either side of the road leading in," Dax added. "The headlights approaching from below seem to have their attention for now."

"Let's move on the trailer guards before the

vehicle arrives," Gus said. "Hunter, you're with me on the lead trailer. Dax and Cliff, you're on the one in the middle. Tony and TJ take the rear trailer guards. Go."

The men eased forward, moving silently through the shadows.

Gus and Hunter came around their trailer at the same time as the others, surprising the guards before they had a chance to raise their weapons. Gus swung the butt of his rifle into the side of one man's head while Hunter smashed his into the other man's face, crushing his nose.

Gus's guy dropped to his knees, clearly stunned. Gus hit him again, and the man fell forward, out cold.

Hunter swept his guy's feet out from under him and pinned him to the ground. While Hunter held him down, Gus secured him with zip ties around his wrists and slapped a piece of duct tape over his mouth.

Gus glanced at the second trailer. Cliff had one guy in a chokehold. Dax had his guy face-down on the ground.

A shout rang out from the last trailer. Whoever emitted it only did it once before Tony and TJ had their guys subdued.

Unfortunately, the shout was enough to alert the two men on the road.

The Brotherhood Protectors faded back into the shadows, leaving the guards lying on the ground.

When the road guards reached the first trailer, they held their guns ready as they approached the pair of guards lying in the dirt.

"What the hell?" one of them said.

Dax stepped out of the shadows near the second trailer. "Hey," he said, "can I bum a smoke?"

The two men raised their weapons. They were so focused on Dax that they didn't hear Gus and Hunter until they were right behind them.

Cliff grabbed one of the guys in a chokehold.

The man's rifle went off, the bullet heading for the stars. As Cliff tightened his hold, the man let go of his weapon and clawed at the arm around his throat.

At the same time Cliff jumped his guy, Gus hit the other man with the stun gun. It wasn't nearly as satisfying as slamming the butt of his weapon into a man's face, but it did the trick. The man fell to his knees.

Gus had him zip-tied and gagged with duct tape before the effects of the stun gun could wear off.

By that time, the headlights on the road below rounded a corner and headed straight for them.

"Hunter, take up a sniper position," Gus said. "The rest of you stand fast in front of each trailer, weapons ready. Maybe they won't notice we aren't their guards until too late."

CHAPTER 18

As Peyton lay on the truck bed, she kept watch on the man perched on the side. His attention was focused on the road ahead, but he occasionally glanced down at their prisoner.

While he was looking away, Peyton curled into the fetal position, pretending to be scared. That wasn't hard, considering she was terrified. With her hands tucked close to her belly, the man above couldn't see that she'd pulled her wrists free of the zip tie or that she was now pushing the boots down while pulling her feet out.

Peyton freed her feet, gripped a boot and waited. When the truck made a sharp turn on the old logging road, she made her move.

She rolled to her knees and swung the boot up at the man beside her with as much force as she could muster. The boot caught him in the face. He teetered backward. Centrifugal force did the rest, and he fell out of the truck.

Peyton slipped over the opposite side of the truck onto gravel. When she landed, she pitched forward, then tucked and rolled into the brush growing up to the edge of the road.

The man she'd knocked off the truck shouted.

The truck ground to a halt, and the two men inside leaped out.

Peyton staggered to her feet and ran into the woods. She didn't get far before the big guy who'd grabbed her out of the crowd at the rodeo caught up with her. He hooked an arm around her waist and carried her back to the truck and Snake.

She kicked and clawed at the arm around her waist to no avail. The man was three times bigger and much stronger than she was.

He dropped her in front of Snake.

When she pushed to her feet, she lifted her chin and glared at the man who'd made her life hell.

"Bitch," he said and backhanded her across her mouth, busting her lip.

Peyton ran her tongue across her lip, tasting the coppery tang of blood. She faced Snake, hate swelling in her heart for this man who had so little regard for other people's lives. "You disgust me," she said through clenched teeth.

"Then you'll be pleased to know you won't have to put up with me for long." Snake pulled a gun out of his belt and pressed the barrel against Peyton's temple. "Since you were so eager to get out on our own, let's walk the rest of the way."

Peyton refused to give him the satisfaction of seeing her in pain.

Snake gave her a shove to get her moving. With one hand holding the gun to her temple, he clamped the other on her shoulder.

She walked across the gravel, the bottoms of her bare feet tender against sharp rocks.

Snake's two sidekicks fell in step beside her, blocking her from escaping yet again. The one she'd hit in the face had a nosebleed, and his eye was swelling.

Peyton couldn't feel sorry for this man or any of the men who worked with Snake. They were the lowest form of life in the world.

The trailers came into view, lined up along the side of the logging trail. This was the end of the road. If a miracle didn't happen soon, she'd failed the women trapped in the trailers.

Where were Gus and the other members of the Brotherhood Protectors? Had the tracking devices stopped working? Had they lost her signal? Was it blocked by mountain peaks?

As they approached the trailers, Snake muttered, "Where the hell are our road guards? Are they taking a fucking smoke break?"

Peyton studied the scene ahead. Three trailers,

armed guards posted in front of each, their faces shadowed. Her skin tingled. Her gut told her to be alert and ready for anything.

Gus stood still when the approaching vehicle suddenly stopped, and the driver and passenger jumped out. The driver, a taller, bulkier man, dove into the woods. Moments later, he emerged and shoved a smaller figure in front of him.

"It's Peyton," Gus said. "Hunter, hold your fire until you have a clear shot."

"Roger," Hunter said from his position somewhere up the hill, shrouded in shadows. If anyone had a chance at picking off Snake, it was Hunter, the best sniper of the Yellowstone team.

Gus wanted to rush forward, shoot the men and take Peyton into his arms. But he couldn't risk it. They were still too far away. If he made a move now, they might get trigger-happy and shoot Peyton. The shorter man who'd been the passenger pointed something at Peyton's head. Then he shoved her forward, toward the trailers. That man had to be Snake, holding a gun to Peyton's temple.

Another man joined them, whose face appeared covered in blood.

As they neared, Gus could tell Peyton was struggling with each step. Anger burned in his chest when he realized she was barefoot, walking across the gravel. He fought the urge to lunge forward and choke the life out of Snake. Instead, he stood fast, waiting for Snake and his two men to come closer with Peyton before his team made a move.

"It's time," Snake called out. "You have your instructions; light 'em up."

Peyton gasped, coming to a full stop. "You can't be serious. There are women inside those trailers."

Snake snorted. "That's the point. I promised that if you escaped again, I'd kill them. And you'll have the pleasure of watching them die because of your selfish desire to leave."

Gus heard every word the man spoke, designed to make Peyton take the blame for the deaths of the women inside the trailers.

"What are you waiting for?" Snake called out. "Torch those trailers."

"It's not going to happen." Gus stepped forward, out of the shadow of the trailer, his AR-15 pointed at the man holding Peyton hostage. "It's over, Snake. Drop your gun and step away from Ms. Running Bear."

"Ah, the infamous Brotherhood Protectors to the rescue. That's right. I know who you are. Ex-SEALSs and Special Operations types. Your fancy training doesn't mean you'll save them all." Snake shook his head. "You didn't save my brother when he was captured in Iraq. You didn't get him out before he was dragged through the country and beheaded."

"Is that what this is all about?" Gus asked. "You're trafficking these women as a way to get back at the government for letting your brother down?"

Snake snorted. "Oh, hell no. A guy's got to make a living. This job pays more than most. It's just a bonus when I can best our government's supposed finest."

"Let her go, Snake. You're not getting away this time," Gus said. "With or without her."

"And you're not listening, man," Snake said. "I can't do that. I don't take orders from you or anyone else. But you'll take orders from me if you don't want me to put a bullet through your girlfriend's head."

"Let her go," Gus said. "Killing her will only add more years to the length of your stay in prison."

"I'm afraid I can't do that." Snake's lips curled back. "You see, this bitch is my ticket out of here. If you don't want to see her pretty face splattered, put down your weapons."

"Don't do it, Gus," Peyton said, her voice low and insistent. "He's going to kill me anyway. Shoot him now. Save yourself, and save the women in those trailers."

"I can't shoot him," Gus said. "I might hit you."

Peyton shook her head. "With or without me, he can't be allowed to roam free. He's dangerous and cruel. If he gets away this time, he'll do it again and put more women through hell."

"I can't shoot through you to get to him," Gus shook his head. "It's not an option."

"You're right," Peyton said, her argument making a complete about-face. "It's too soon." She was using words he'd said to her when they'd come close to making love.

Gus tensed. "Hunter, be ready," he whispered, hoping the radio picked up his words.

Peyton continued. "And when you know it's right, you go for it." She stared at him. "It's right. Now."

Peyton pulled something from her back pocket and slammed it into Snake's leg.

Gus grinned. She'd used the stun gun. The woman was brilliant,

Snake released his hold on Peyton and sank to the ground, falling forward onto his face.

A shot rang out.

"Don't move, or we'll shoot," Gus shouted.

The two men closest to Peyton raised their hands in surrender.

Dax and Cliff hurried to secure Snake and his other two minions.

Gus crossed to Peyton, pulled her into his arms and held her for a long time. "I lost several years of my life while he had the gun pointed at your head."

Peyton nodded. "I was afraid he'd shoot you."

"I guess it just wasn't our day to die." Gus lifted her hand to his lips and pressed a kiss to the inside of her palm. "Come on. Let's help the ladies you came to save."

"Thank you," Peyton said. "You didn't have to help

me save them. But you did. For that, you hold a very special place in my heart."

"Sweetheart, you hold my whole heart." Gus bent to brush his lips across hers. For a long moment, they held each other. Safe from harm. They hadn't been too late.

An SUV arrived near the trailers. Stone and the rest of the team got out.

"Well, damn," Carter Manning said. "We missed the party."

Stone approached Gus and Peyton.

"The threat has been neutralized," Gus reported. "We just need to unlock the trailers and get those women out."

Stoned nodded. "Good job." He smiled at Peyton. "I'm glad to see you're okay. We were worried when you disappeared from the rodeo."

Peyton stood in the curve of Gus's arm. "Thankfully, you found us." She tipped her head toward Snake, who was just coming out of the effects of the stun gun. "You might find the trailer keys in that man's pocket. He keeps them on a big key ring."

Stone passed that information on to one of the other men and then turned back to Gus and Peyton. "The sheriff's department has been notified. They're sending ambulances to collect the women. They'll be transported to the hospital in Bozeman."

Gus and Peyton watched as the trailers were unlocked one by one.

"They're not going to know what's going on," Peyton said. "They keep them drugged."

"Maybe that's a good thing," Gus said, "until they can be transported to a safe location."

Stone stood beside Peyton. "They called in a team of health care professionals to help, including mental health professionals trained to work with victims of sexual abuse. We also notified the FBI's Human Trafficking Unit. They're trained to work with the victims."

"Good," Peyton said. "They'll need all the help they can get to reclaim the lives they lost."

Sheriff's vehicles and ambulances arrived. Stone left Gus and Peyton to greet them.

Peyton slipped her arm around Gus's waist. "It's finally over."

His arm tightened around her. "Yes, this part is." Reaching up, he removed his earbuds. Then he turned her in his arms and stared down at her in the starlight. "But I'm not ready for us to be over."

"No?" she said, staring up at him, the starlight reflecting off the tears welling in her eyes.

"I'm not ready for us to be over..." he said softly, "*ever.*"

The tears slipped down her cheeks. "Are you sure? I mean, I'm not...I've been...so many..." She looked away, unable to form the words she needed to warn him about what he was getting into. "I'm damaged goods."

He tipped her chin up and brushed the tears from her cheeks. "You're the bravest woman I've ever known. And you have a heart as big as the Montana sky." He brushed his lips across hers. "That makes you perfect."

"I have panic attacks," she reminded him.

He grinned. "So do I. We'll work through them."

"What if I have one while we're..."

"Making love?" He met and held her gaze. "We'll take it slow, get to know each other, go on dates. We'll start with a kiss." He showed her with a gentle kiss.

"I like that," she said and leaned up to kiss him again.

"I can be patient," he said.

"Mmm," she said and grinned. "I might not be so much."

Gus laughed and hugged her close.

EPILOGUE

Two months later.

"Can you help me move the sofa?" Peyton stood beside the sofa Hank and Sadie had given them as a housewarming gift for the cottage they'd rented in Bozeman.

Gus entered the living room, set his beer on the coffee table and took a position at the other end of the couch. "I thought this was where you wanted it?"

She grimaced. "It was." She grimaced. "But I changed my mind. I forgot that I needed to make room for my desk behind it. We don't have to move it far, just enough."

"When does your desk arrive?" Gus asked as he lifted his end of the sofa at the same time as Peyton lifted hers.

Peyton didn't answer until they'd set the heavy piece in the new position. Then she straightened and grinned. "It arrives as soon as we pick it up from the furniture store."

Gus closed the distance between them and pulled her into his arms. "What happened to taking a day off?"

She wrapped her arms around his neck and stared up into the eyes of the man she was falling in love with more each day. "This is our day off," she said. "I finished my homework last night. All we have to do today is pick up my desk, and the rest of the day is ours to do..." she ran her finger down his naked chest, "whatever we want to do."

He captured her hand in his and brought it to his lips. "Could we start with the whatever we want to do and then get the desk?"

She tilted her head, lowered her lashes and purred, "Mmm. I could be convinced."

"Here on the couch?" He dropped onto the sofa, pulling her down onto his lap.

"A distinct possibility." She straddled him and bent to press her lips to his. "As long as I get to be on top this time."

"Your wish is my command," he said as he dragged her T-shirt over her head and tossed it across the lampshade.

When he reached behind her for the clasp on her

bra, he fumbled for a moment until she brushed his hands aside and undid it herself.

"I like the ones that fasten in the front," he said, sliding the straps from her shoulders.

She chuckled. "I'll remember that. I must make things easy for the Navy SEAL."

He cocked an eyebrow. "Are you patronizing me?"

She gave him half a smile. "Maybe. I need practice managing difficult patients."

Gus cupped her breasts in his hands. "You're going to be a terrific nurse." He leaned forward and took one of her breasts into his mouth, flicking the tip with his tongue until it tightened into a little bead.

"Mmm. You're my kind of patient."

Gus nipped the bud. "As long as you don't treat any others like this."

"No way," she said, cupping his cheeks between her palms. "I'm a one-man-woman, and you're the man for me."

"Good thing, too," he said. "Because I'm in love with you, and I can't imagine a day without you in it."

She smiled down at him, her heart full to overflowing. "I'm beyond blessed and don't know how life could be better than it is right now."

"Sweetheart, as long as we're together, it'll just get better and better. And to think it all started when I fell off a haystack onto you." He laughed. "Luckiest day of my life."

"And mine," Peyton said. "Now, show me how much you love me. Make love to me. Here. Now. Forever."

THE END

THANK you for reading SAVING PEYTON. The Brotherhood Protectors Yellowstone Series continues with Saving Londyn.

BREAKING SILENCE

DELTA FORCE STRONG BOOK #1

New York Times & USA Today
Bestselling Author

ELLE JAMES

BREAKING
Silence

DELTA FORCE
STRONG

New York Times & *USA Today* Bestselling Author
ELLE JAMES

CHAPTER 1

HAD he known they would be deployed so soon after their last short mission to El Salvador, Rucker Sloan wouldn't have bought that dirt bike from his friend Duff. Now, it would sit there for months before he actually got to take it out to the track.

The team had been given forty-eight hours to pack their shit, take care of business and get onto the C130 that would transport them to Afghanistan.

Now, boots on the ground, duffel bags stowed in their assigned quarters behind the wire, they were ready to take on any mission the powers that be saw fit to assign.

What he wanted most that morning, after being awake for the past thirty-six hours, was a cup of strong, black coffee.

The rest of his team had hit the sack as soon as they got in. Rucker had already met with their commanding officer, gotten a brief introduction to the regional issues and had been told to get some rest. They'd be operational within the next forty-eight hours.

Too wound up to sleep, Rucker followed a stream of people he hoped were heading for the chow hall. He should be able to get coffee there.

On the way, he passed a sand volleyball court where two teams played against each other. One of the teams had four players, the other only three. The four-person squad slammed a ball to the ground on the other side of the net. The only female player ran after it as it rolled toward Rucker.

He stopped the ball with his foot and picked it up.

The woman was tall, slender, blond-haired and blue-eyed. She wore an Army PT uniform of shorts and an Army T-shirt with her hair secured back from her face in a ponytail seated on the crown of her head.

Without makeup, and sporting a sheen of perspiration, she was sexy as hell, and the men on both teams knew it.

They groaned when Rucker handed her the ball. He'd robbed them of watching the female soldier bending over to retrieve the runaway.

She took the ball and frowned. "Do you play?"

"I have," he answered.

"We could use a fourth." She lifted her chin in challenge.

Tired from being awake for the past thirty-six hours, Rucker opened his mouth to say *hell no*. But he made the mistake of looking into her sky-blue eyes and instead said, "I'm in."

What the hell was he thinking?

Well, hadn't he been wound up from too many hours sitting in transit? What he needed was a little physical activity to relax his mind and muscles. At least, that's what he told himself in the split-second it took to step into the sandbox and serve up a heaping helping of whoop-ass.

He served six times before the team playing opposite finally returned one. In between each serve, his side gave him high-fives, all members except one—the blonde with the blue eyes he stood behind, admiring the length of her legs beneath her black Army PT shorts.

Twenty minutes later, Rucker's team won the match. The teams broke up and scattered to get showers or breakfast in the chow hall.

"Can I buy you a cup of coffee?" the pretty blonde asked.

"Only if you tell me your name." He twisted his lips into a wry grin. "I'd like to know who delivered those wicked spikes."

She held out her hand. "Nora Michaels," she said.

He gripped her hand in his, pleased to feel firm pressure. Women might be the weaker sex, but he didn't like a dead fish handshake from males or females. Firm and confident was what he preferred. Like her ass in those shorts.

She cocked an eyebrow. "And you are?"

He'd been so intent thinking about her legs and ass, he'd forgotten to introduce himself. "Rucker Sloan. Just got in less than an hour ago."

"Then you could probably use a tour guide to the nearest coffee."

He nodded. "Running on fumes here. Good coffee will help."

"I don't know about good, but it's coffee and it's fresh." She released his hand and fell in step beside him, heading in the direction of some of the others from their volleyball game.

"As long as it's strong and black, I'll be happy."

She laughed. "And awake for the next twenty-four hours."

"Spoken from experience?" he asked, casting a glance in her direction.

She nodded. "I work nights in the medical facility. It can be really boring and hard to stay awake when we don't have any patients to look after." She held up her hands. "Not that I want any of our boys injured and in need of our care."

"But it does get boring," he guessed.

"It makes for a long deployment." She held out her hand. "Nice to meet you, Rucker. Is Rucker a call sign or your real name?"

He grinned. "Real name. That was the only thing

my father gave me before he cut out and left my mother and me to make it on our own."

"Your mother raised you, and you still joined the Army?" She raised an eyebrow. "Most mothers don't want their boys to go off to war."

"It was that or join a gang and end up dead in a gutter," he said. "She couldn't afford to send me to college. I was headed down the gang path when she gave me the ultimatum. Join and get the GI-Bill, or she would cut me off and I'd be out in the streets. To her, it was the only way to get me out of L.A. and to have the potential to go to college someday."

She smiled "And you stayed in the military."

He nodded. "I found a brotherhood that was better than any gang membership in LA. For now, I take college classes online. It was my mother's dream for me to graduate college. She never went, and she wanted so much more for me than the streets of L.A.. When my gig is up with the Army, if I haven't finished my degree, I'll go to college fulltime."

"And major in what?" Nora asked.

"Business management. I'm going to own my own security service. I want to put my combat skills to use helping people who need dedicated and specialized protection."

Nora nodded. "Sounds like a good plan."

"I know the protection side of things. I need to learn the business side and business law. Life will be different on the civilian side."

"True."

"How about you? What made you sign up?" he asked.

She shrugged. "I wanted to put my nursing degree to good use and help our men and women in uniform. This is my first assignment after training."

"Drinking from the firehose?" Rucker stopped in front of the door to the mess hall.

She nodded. "Yes. But it's the best baptism under fire medical personnel can get. I'll be a better nurse for it when I return to the States."

"How much longer do you have to go?" he asked, hoping that she'd say she'd be there as long as he was. In his case, he never knew how long their deployments would last. One week, one month, six months…

She gave him a lopsided smile. "I ship out in a week."

"That's too bad." He opened the door for her. "I just got here. That doesn't give us much time to get to know each other."

"That's just as well." Nora stepped through the door. "I don't want to be accused of fraternizing. I'm too close to going back to spoil my record."

Rucker chuckled. "Playing volleyball and sharing a table while drinking coffee won't get you written up. I like the way you play. I'm curious to know where you learned to spike like that."

"I guess that's reasonable. Coffee first." She led him into the chow hall.

The smells of food and coffee made Rucker's mouth water.

He grabbed a tray and loaded his plate with eggs, toast and pancakes drenched in syrup. Last, he stopped at the coffee urn and filled his cup with freshly brewed black coffee.

When he looked around, he found Nora seated at one of the tables, holding a mug in her hands, a small plate with cottage cheese and peaches on it.

He strode over to her. "Mind if I join you?"

"As long as you don't hit on me," she said with cocked eyebrows.

"You say that as if you've been hit on before."

She nodded and sipped her steaming brew. "I lost count how many times in the first week I was here."

"Shows they have good taste in women and, unfortunately, limited manners."

"And you're better?" she asked, a smile twitching the corners of her lips.

"I'm not hitting on you. You can tell me to leave, and I'll be out of this chair so fast, you won't have time to enunciate the V."

She stared straight into his eyes, canted her head to one side and said, "Leave."

In the middle of cutting into one of his pancakes, Rucker dropped his knife and fork on the tray, shot out of his chair and left with his tray, sloshing coffee as he moved. He hoped she was just testing him. If she wasn't...oh, well. He was used to eating meals alone. If she was, she'd have to come to him.

He took a seat at the next table, his back to her, and resumed cutting into his pancake.

Nora didn't utter a word behind him.

Oh, well. He popped a bite of syrupy sweet pancake in his mouth and chewed thoughtfully. She was only there for another week. Man, she had a nice ass...and those legs... He sighed and bent over his plate to stab his fork into a sausage link.

"This chair taken?" a soft, female voice sounded in front of him.

He looked up to see the pretty blond nurse standing there with her tray in her hands, a crooked smile on her face.

He lifted his chin in silent acknowledgement.

She laid her tray on the table and settled onto the chair. "I didn't think you'd do it."

"Fair enough. You don't know me," he said.

"I know that you joined the Army to get out of street life. That your mother raised you after your father skipped out, that you're working toward a business degree and that your name is Rucker." She sipped her coffee.

He nodded, secretly pleased she'd remembered all that. Maybe there was hope for getting to know the pretty nurse before she redeployed to the States. And who knew? They might run into each other on the other side of the pond.

Still, he couldn't show too much interest, or he'd be no better than the other guys who'd hit on her. "Since you're redeploying back to the States in a week, and I'm due to go out on a mission, probably within the next twenty-four to forty-eight hours, I don't know if it's worth our time to get to know each other any more than we already have."

She nodded. "I guess that's why I want to sit with you. You're not a danger to my perfect record of no fraternizing. I don't have to worry that you'll fall in love with me in such a short amount of time." She winked.

He chuckled. "As I'm sure half of this base has fallen in love with you since you've been here."

She shrugged. "I don't know if it's love, but it's damned annoying."

"How so?"

She rolled her eyes toward the ceiling. "I get flowers left on my door every day."

"And that's annoying? I'm sure it's not easy coming up with flowers out here in the desert." He set down his fork and took up his coffee mug. "I think it's sweet." He held back a smile. Well, almost.

"They're hand-drawn on notepad paper and left on the door of my quarters and on the door to the shower tent." She shook her head. "It's kind of creepy and stalkerish."

Rucker nodded. "I see your point. The guys should at least have tried their hands at origami flowers, since the real things are scarce around here."

Nora smiled. "I'm not worried about the pictures, but the line for sick call is ridiculous."

"How so?"

"So many of the guys come up with the lamest excuses to come in and hit on me. I asked to work the nightshift to avoid sick call altogether."

"You have a fan group." He smiled. "Has the adoration gone to your head?"

She snorted softly. "No."

"You didn't get this kind of reaction back in the States?"

"I haven't been on active duty for long. I only decided to join the Army after my mother passed away. I was her fulltime nurse for a couple years as she went through stage four breast cancer. We thought she might make it." Her shoulders sagged. "But she didn't."

"I'm sorry to hear that. My mother meant a lot to me, as well. I sent money home every month after I enlisted and kept sending it up until the day she died suddenly of an aneurysm."

"I'm so sorry about your mother's passing," Nora said, shaking her head. "Wow. As an enlisted man, how did you make enough to send some home?"

"I ate in the chow hall and lived on post. I didn't

party or spend money on civilian clothes or booze. Mom needed it. I gave it to her."

"You were a good son to her," Nora said.

His chest tightened. "She died of an aneurysm a couple of weeks before she was due to move to Texas where I'd purchased a house for her."

"Wow. And, let me guess, you blame yourself for not getting her to Texas sooner...?" Her gaze captured his.

Her words hit home, and he winced. "Yeah. I should've done it sooner."

"Can't bring people back with regrets." Nora stared into her coffee cup. "I learned that. The only thing I could do was move forward and get on with living. I wanted to get away from Milwaukee and the home I'd shared with my mother. Not knowing where else to go, I wandered past a realtor's office and stepped into a recruiter's office. I had my nursing degree, they wanted and needed nurses on active duty. I signed up, they put me through some officer training and here I am." She held her arms out.

"Playing volleyball in Afghanistan, working on your tan during the day and helping soldiers at night." Rucker gave her a brief smile. "I, for one, appreciate what you're doing for our guys and gals."

"I do the best I can," she said softly. "I just wish I could do more. I'd rather stay here than redeploy back to the States, but they're afraid if they keep us here too long, we'll burn out or get PTSD."

"One week, huh?"

She nodded. "One week."

"In my field, one week to redeploy back to the States is a dangerous time. Anything can happen and usually does."

"Yeah, but you guys are on the frontlines, if not behind enemy lines. I'm back here. What could happen?"

Rucker flinched. "Oh, sweetheart, you didn't just say that…" He glanced around, hoping no one heard her tempt fate with those dreaded words *What could happen?*

Nora grinned. "You're not superstitious, are you?"

"In what we do, we can't afford not to be," he said, tossing salt over his shoulder.

"I'll be fine," she said in a reassuring, nurse's voice.

"Stop," he said, holding up his hand. "You're only digging the hole deeper." He tossed more salt over his other shoulder.

Nora laughed.

"Don't laugh." He handed her the saltshaker. "Do it."

"I'm not tossing salt over my shoulder. Someone has to clean the mess hall."

Rucker leaned close and shook salt over her shoulder. "I don't know if it counts if someone else throws salt over your shoulder, but I figure you now need every bit of luck you can get."

"You're a fighter but afraid of a little bad luck."

Nora shook her head. "Those two things don't seem to go together."

"You'd be surprised how easily my guys are freaked by the littlest things."

"And you," she reminded him.

"You asking *what could happen?* isn't a little thing. That's in-your-face tempting fate." Rucker was laying it on thick to keep her grinning, but deep down, he believed what he was saying. And it didn't make a difference the amount of education he had or the statistics that predicted outcomes. His gut told him she'd just tempted fate with her statement. Maybe he was overthinking things. Now, he was worried she wouldn't make it back to the States alive.

NORA LIKED RUCKER. He was the first guy who'd walked away without an argument since she'd arrived at the base in Afghanistan. He'd meant what he'd said and proved it. His dark brown hair and deep green eyes, coupled with broad shoulders and a narrow waist, made him even more attractive. Not all the men were in as good a shape as Rucker. And he seemed to have a very determined attitude.

She hadn't known what to expect when she'd deployed. Being the center of attention of almost every single male on the base hadn't been one of her expectations. She'd only ever considered herself average in the looks department. But when the men outnumbered women by more than ten to one, she guessed average appearance moved up in the ranks.

"Where did you learn to play volleyball?" Rucker asked, changing the subject of her leaving and her flippant comment about what could happen in one week.

"I was on the volleyball team in high school. It got me a scholarship to a small university in my home state of Minnesota, where I got my Bachelor of Science degree in Nursing."

"It takes someone special to be a nurse," he stated. "Is that what you always wanted to be?"

She shook her head. "I wanted to be a firefighter when I was in high school."

"What made you change your mind?"

She stared down at the coffee growing cold in her mug. "My mother was diagnosed with cancer when I was a senior in high school. I wanted to help but felt like I didn't know enough to be of assistance." She looked up. "She made it through chemo and radiation treatments and still came to all of my volleyball games. I thought she was in the clear."

"She wasn't?" Rucker asked, his tone low and gentle.

"She didn't tell me any different. When I got the scholarship, I told her I wanted to stay close to home to be with her. She insisted I go and play volleyball for the university. I was pretty good and played for the first two years I was there. I quit the team in my third year to start the nursing program. I didn't know there was anything wrong back home. I called every week to talk to Mom. She never let on that she was sick." She forced a smile. "But you don't want my sob story. You probably want to know what's going on around here."

He set his mug on the table. "If we were alone in a coffee bar back in the States, I'd reach across the table and take your hand."

"Oh, please. Don't do that." She looked around the mess hall, half expecting someone might have overheard Rucker's comment. "You're enlisted. I'm an officer. That would get us into a whole lot of trouble."

"Yeah, but we're also two human beings. I wouldn't be human if I didn't feel empathy for you and want to provide comfort."

She set her coffee cup on the table and laid her hands in her lap. "I'll be satisfied with the thought. Thank you."

"Doesn't seem like enough. When did you find out your mother was sick?"

She swallowed the sadness that welled in her throat every time she remembered coming home to find out her mother had been keeping her illness from her. "It wasn't until I went home for Christmas in my senior year that I realized she'd been lying to me for a while." She laughed in lieu of sobbing. "I don't care who they are, old people don't always tell the truth."

"How long had she been keeping her sickness from you?"

"She'd known the cancer had returned halfway through my junior year. I hadn't gone home that summer because I'd been working hard to get my coursework and clinical hours in the nursing program. When I went home at Christmas…" Nora gulped. "She wasn't the same person. She'd lost so much weight and looked twenty years older."

"Did you stay home that last semester?" Rucker asked.

"Mom insisted I go back to school and finish what I'd started. Like your mother, she hadn't gone to college. She wanted her only child to graduate. She was afraid that if I stayed home to take care of her, I wouldn't finish my nursing degree."

"I heard from a buddy of mine that those programs can be hard to get into," he said. "I can see why she wouldn't want you to drop everything in your life to take care of her."

Nora gave him a watery smile. "That's what she said. As soon as my last final was over, I returned to my hometown. I became her nurse. She lasted another three months before she slipped away."

"That's when you joined the Army?"

She shook her head. "Dad was so heartbroken, I stayed a few months until he was feeling better. I got a job at a local emergency room. On weekends, my father and I worked on cleaning out the house and getting it ready to put on the market."

"Is your dad still alive?" Rucker asked.

Nora nodded. "He lives in Texas. He moved to a small house with a big backyard." She forced a smile. "He has a garden, and all the ladies in his retirement community think he's the cat's meow. He still misses Mom, but he's getting on with his life."

Rucker tilted his head. "When did you join the military?"

"When Dad sold the house and moved into his retirement community. I worried about him, but he's doing better."

"And you?"

"I miss her. But she'd whip my ass if I wallowed in self-pity for more than a moment. She was a strong woman and expected me to be the same."

Rucker grinned. "From what I've seen, you are."

Nora gave him a skeptical look. "You've only seen me playing volleyball. It's just a game." Not that she'd admit it, but she was a real softy when it came to caring for the sick and injured.

"If you're half as good at nursing, which I'm willing to bet you are, you're amazing." He started to reach across the table for her hand. Before he actually touched her, he grabbed the saltshaker and shook it over his cold breakfast.

"You just got in this morning?" Nora asked.

Rucker nodded.

"How long will you be here?" she asked.

"I don't know."

"What do you mean, you don't know? I thought when people were deployed, they were given a specific timeframe."

"Most people are. We're deployed where and when needed."

Nora frowned. "What are you? Some kind of special forces team?"

His lips pressed together. "Can't say."

She sat back. He was some kind of Special Forces. "Army, right?"

He nodded.

That would make him Delta Force. The elite of the elite. A very skilled soldier who undertook incredibly dangerous missions. She gulped and stopped herself from reaching across the table to take his hand. "Well, I hope all goes well while you and your team are here."

"Thanks."

A man hurried across the chow hall wearing shorts and an Army T-shirt. He headed directly toward their table.

Nora didn't recognize him. "Expecting someone?" she asked Rucker, tipping her head toward the man.

Rucker turned, a frown pulling his eyebrows together. "Why the hell's Dash awake?"

Nora frowned. "Dash? Please tell me that's his callsign, not his real name."

Rucker laughed. "It should be his real name. He's first into the fight, and he's fast." Rucker stood and faced his teammate. "What's up?"

"CO wants us all in the Tactical Operations Center," Dash said. "On the double."

"Guess that's my cue to exit." Rucker turned to Nora. "I enjoyed our talk."

She nodded. "Me, too."

Dash grinned. "Tell you what…I'll stay and finish your conversation while you see what the commander wants."

Rucker hooked Dash's arm twisted it up behind his back, and gave him a shove toward the door. "You heard the CO, he wants all of us." Rucker winked at Nora. "I hope to see you on the volleyball court before you leave."

"Same. Good luck." Nora's gaze followed Rucker's broad shoulders and tight ass out of the chow hall. Too bad she'd only be there another week before she shipped out. She would've enjoyed more volleyball and coffee with the Delta Force operative.

He'd probably be on maneuvers that entire week.

She stacked her tray and coffee cup in the collection area and left the chow hall, heading for the building where she shared her quarters with Beth Drennan, a nurse she'd become friends with during their deployment together.

As close as they were, Nora didn't bring up her conversation with the Delta. With only a week left at the base, she probably wouldn't run into him again. Though she would like to see him again, she prayed he didn't end up in the hospital.

ABOUT THE AUTHOR

ELLE JAMES also writing as MYLA JACKSON is a *New York Times* and *USA Today* Bestselling author of books including cowboys, intrigues and paranormal adventures that keep her readers on the edges of their seats. When she's not at her computer, she's traveling, snow skiing, boating, or riding her ATV, dreaming up new stories. Learn more about Elle James at www.ellejames.com

Website | Facebook | Twitter | GoodReads | Newsletter | BookBub | Amazon

Or visit her alter ego Myla Jackson at mylajackson.com
Website | Facebook | Twitter | Newsletter

Follow Me!
www.ellejames.com
ellejamesauthor@gmail.com

ALSO BY ELLE JAMES

Brotherhood Protectors Boxed Set 6

Shadow Assassin

Iron Horse Legacy

Soldier's Duty (#1)

Ranger's Baby (#2)

Marine's Promise (#3)

SEAL's Vow (#4)

Warrior's Resolve (#5)

Drake (#6)

Grimm (#7)

Murdock (#8)

Utah (#9)

Judge (#10)

Delta Force Strong

Ivy's Delta (Delta Force 3 Crossover)

Breaking Silence (#1)

Breaking Rules (#2)

Breaking Away (#3)

Breaking Free (#4)

Breaking Hearts (#5)

Breaking Ties (#6)

Breaking Point (#7)

SEAL'S Defiance (#7)

SEAL's Deception (#8)

SEAL's Deliverance (#9)

SEAL's Ultimate Challenge (#10)

Texas Billionaire Club

Tarzan & Janine (#1)

Something To Talk About (#2)

Who's Your Daddy (#3)

Love & War (#4)

Billionaire Online Dating Service

The Billionaire Husband Test (#1)

The Billionaire Cinderella Test (#2)

The Billionaire Bride Test (#3)

The Billionaire Daddy Test (#4)

The Billionaire Matchmaker Test (#5)

The Billionaire Glitch Date (#6)

The Billionaire Perfect Date (#7) coming soon

The Billionaire Replacement Date (#8) coming soon

The Billionaire Wedding Date (#9) coming soon

Cajun Magic Mystery Series

Voodoo on the Bayou (#1)

Voodoo for Two (#2)

Deja Voodoo (#3)

Cajun Magic Mysteries Books 1-3

The Outriders

Homicide at Whiskey Gulch (#1)

Hideout at Whiskey Gulch (#2)

Held Hostage at Whiskey Gulch (#3)

Setup at Whiskey Gulch (#4)

Missing Witness at Whiskey Gulch (#5)

Cowboy Justice at Whiskey Gulch (#6)

Ballistic Cowboy

Hot Combat (#1)

Hot Target (#2)

Hot Zone (#3)

Hot Velocity (#4)

Declan's Defenders

Marine Force Recon (#1)

Show of Force (#2)

Full Force (#3)

Driving Force (#4)

Tactical Force (#5)

Disruptive Force (#6)

Mission: Six

One Intrepid SEAL

Two Dauntless Hearts

Three Courageous Words

Four Relentless Days

Five Ways to Surrender

Six Minutes to Midnight

SEAL Of My Own

Navy SEAL Survival

Navy SEAL Captive

Navy SEAL To Die For

Navy SEAL Six Pack

Devil's Shroud Series

Deadly Reckoning (#1)

Deadly Engagement (#2)

Deadly Liaisons (#3)

Deadly Allure (#4)

Deadly Obsession (#5)

Deadly Fall (#6)

Covert Cowboys Inc Series

Triggered (#1)

Taking Aim (#2)

Bodyguard Under Fire (#3)

Cowboy Resurrected (#4)

Navy SEAL Justice (#5)

Navy SEAL Newlywed (#6)

High Country Hideout (#7)

Clandestine Christmas (#8)

Thunder Horse Series

Hostage to Thunder Horse (#1)

Thunder Horse Heritage (#2)

Thunder Horse Redemption (#3)

Christmas at Thunder Horse Ranch (#4)

Demon Series

Hot Demon Nights (#1)

Demon's Embrace (#2)

Tempting the Demon (#3)

Lords of the Underworld

Witch's Initiation (#1)

Witch's Seduction (#2)

The Witch's Desire (#3)

Possessing the Witch (#4)

Stealth Operations Specialists (SOS)

Nick of Time

Alaskan Fantasy

Boys Behaving Badly Anthologies

Rogues (#1)

Blue Collar (#2)

Pirates (#3)

Stranded (#4)

First Responder (#5)

Silver Soldier's (#6)

Blown Away

Warrior's Conquest

Enslaved by the Viking Short Story

Conquests

Smokin' Hot Firemen

Protecting the Colton Bride

Protecting the Colton Bride & Colton's Cowboy Code

Heir to Murder

Secret Service Rescue

High Octane Heroes

Haunted

Engaged with the Boss

Cowboy Brigade

Time Raiders: The Whisper

Bundle of Trouble

Killer Body

Operation XOXO

An Unexpected Clue

Baby Bling

Under Suspicion, With Child

Texas-Size Secrets

Cowboy Sanctuary

Lakota Baby

Dakota Meltdown

Beneath the Texas Moon

Made in United States
Orlando, FL
24 September 2024

51910760R00163